BLOKES ON A PLANE

WHEREFORE ART THOU, JIMBO?

WINDY MOUNTAIN
BOOK 2

JOHN MARTIN

ABOUT THE AUTHOR

John Martin is an Australian. He used to be a journalist, now he's free to be frivolous.

https://johnmartin-author.blog

CONTENTS

ONE
FOREVER IN BLUE GENES

HUDDLED TOGETHER ON THE BENCH, the two old blokes were poring over the specials in the Roses Supermarket catalogue when a shadow dimmed their light. Oodles looked up to find the Mayor, of all people, blocking out the sun.

James Northan, briefcase in hand and wearing a pinstripe suit as though he were on the way to the office he no longer had, smiled snidely.

Oodles was flabbergasted. But he knew the big man beside him would react more explosively.

James had avoided talking to him and Wish-Wash for more than 15 months, quite a feat in a town as small as Windy Mountain. They hadn't even seen him at this end of town.

Sure enough, Wish-Wash scowled and thrust out his chin. "Are you lost, Jimbo?"

James sighed loudly as he tilted his head downwards and flicked a piece of lint from his lapel. "Why must thou always have to be so prickly, Bert?"

The reason he called him Bert was that Wish-Wash was his nickname, and James Northan thought nicknames were crass. The big man's full name was Bert Whish-Willson, and he was 82, one year older than James Northan, who had been the actual mayor years ago. People sometimes called him the Mayor nickname because he still behaved like he was.

Oodles's full name was Clarence Noodle. He was 85.

James Northan looked from man to man. "Methinks the time hast just come for us to bury the hatchet."

"Bring it here then, and I'll bury it in your head—maybe it'll stop you from talking funny, too."

James stepped back sharply. "Did you hear that, Clarence? Bert is threatening me with violence."

Oodles sighed. "I didn't hear anything, James. Except, like him, you talking funny."

"I forgot you two are as thick as thieves."

Wish-Wash bounced to his feet with a flash of yellow shirt and the kind of vigour Oodles hadn't seen from him in years. "I'm sick of you calling me thick."

Oodles quickly levered himself up using the armrest and stepped between them, mainly to hold back Wish-Wash.

This wasn't the first time the three oldest men left in the town had nearly come to blows.

Oodles and Wish-Wash were the unlikely owners of the Tasmanian Tiger Museum across the road from the bench where they had been sitting in the sun taking their mid-morning break.

The Mayor had only set foot in that museum once, and that hadn't ended happily for him.

Oodles, dressed in his usual grey overalls, battled to hold Wish-Wash back. "If you've come here to sign my plaster cast, James, you're too late. Doc Jenkins removed it ages ago."

"Thank goodness for that. I don't give my autograph to any damn fool. I'm not about to reward someone careless enough to break his leg. No, I just thought I would buy you both a cup of tea, for old time's sake."

Wish-Wash jabbed a finger over Oodles's shoulder. "I've never known you to do nothing for nothing."

"People change." James tapped his briefcase. "I thought you both might like to see one of the advertisements in this magazine I've come across."

Oodles exchanged a glance with Bert before they fell in line behind the Mayor. James strode ahead as if he were leading them into battle. On the way, Oodles threw the Roses Supermarket catalogue into a roadside bin.

"What's the bet this is another one of his hare-brained schemes?" Wish-Wash said.

"Oh, guaranteed," Oodles replied.

They reached the Wind Tunnel Cafe at the other end of the High Street.

Wendy, the blonde, middle-aged waitress, looked up as they came through the door. "Would you look at this? Someone's put the band back together!"

The Mayor put his briefcase down next to one of the two tables and wrung his hands as he sat down. "Tea for three, Wendy, dear."

Oodles and Bert sat down opposite him as James clicked open the briefcase. He laid a glossy magazine down on the dappled-red laminate table, flipped through the pages, then turned it towards them.

Oodles frowned. "So what's this all about?"

James stabbed at an advertisement. "Did you know scientists can trace your ancestry through DNA?"

"Can they?" Wish-Wash scratched his head.

"Not from dandruff, you cream-faced loon!" James said. "They take a swab from inside your mouth."

"Gawdsake!" Oodles said. "Why would I want to volunteer my DNA anyway? That's how they build evidence against criminals."

James gave him a disapproving look. "Dost thou have something to hide? Like convict ancestry?"

"Oh, I see what's happening here. You want to prove your lineage goes back to someone famous with pure British blood, who spoke in the same stupid way that you are doing now, and you want to out Wish-Wash and me as being descended from petty Irish criminals."

"Are you?"

"Don't know, don't care," Oodles said.

Wish-Wash blew out his cheeks. "I wouldn't mind having a convict in my closet."

"You don't know your lineage?" James asked.

"Are you kidding?" Wish-Wash ran a hand down one side of his unshaven face. "I don't even know who my father was. Not really."

James turned towards Oodles. "What about you? Any idea?"

Oodles shook his head slowly. "Noodle is an anglicised name. But from what, I can't tell you. All I know is my grandparents arrived on a ship. The ship might have left from Ireland, but more likely it came from Ukraine or somewhere."

"I'll pay for the DNA test, if that's what you're worried about."

"You'll also pay for me?" Wish-Wash said.

"That's what I said, didn't I?"

Wish-Wash held up the magazine. "It says here a lucky entrant will win a trip for two, all expenses paid, to the area their ancestors came from."

James snatched it back and scanned it. "So it does."

"So if you pay for me to take the test, and I win the trip, will I have to take you?"

James sighed. "Let's not get ahead of ourselves, Bert."

Wish-Wash grinned. "But what if I do?"

"That is very unlikely, Bert. But if it doth happen, thou mayest take whoever thou willst. Just not me."

TWO
I HEAR YOU KNOCKING
SOME MONTHS LATER

OODLES SAT bolt upright in bed and looked around the room trying to get his bearings.

His heart was pounding and his flannel pyjamas were sticking to him.

He realised after a few seconds he'd been having a nightmare and the banging was actually coming from the front door.

"Hold your horses, I'm coming." He slid out of bed, grabbed his dressing gown from a bed knob and put on his slippers.

He shuffled past the grandfather clock in the hall, which is when he saw the time. Gawdsake! Who'd be visiting at 7.15 on a Monday morning?

Knock-knock, knock-knock.

When he opened up, his eyes were assaulted by a familiar blaze of colour.

"Seriously?" Oodles blinked against the flood of light. "I just had a dream about you."

"Tacky!" Wish-Wash said.

"It wasn't that kind of dream, you muppet. I dreamt Father

O'Boring was conducting your funeral. You should have seen his face when he heard knocking coming up from your coffin."

Wish-Wash grinned broadly.

Wish-Wash was a large man with skin the colour of linseed putty. He had shaved off his beard again but, as usual, he had missed clumps of whiskers. This was probably accidental but there was the possibility he thought these outcrops could disguise his double-chin, or at least draw attention away from it.

He was dressed as outlandishly as ever, wearing a tie with slanting stripes and a shirt with rainbow-coloured horizontal hoops.

He lived in the flat above the museum premises, so what was he doing here at this time of the morning?

"I've won a holiday to Ireland," Wish-Wash blurted. "I want you to come on the trip with me."

———

Oodles shook his head as he spooned tea from the caddy into the teapot on the kitchen sink. "You've never even been on a plane. Ever heard of Melbourne? Sydney? Somewhere closer?"

"No need to get stroppy. The tickets are for Ireland. You might have won them instead of me if you hadn't been such a pigheaded old man."

"Who are you calling old? I'm less than three years older than you!"

It was a tight squeeze in the cramped kitchen, and probably a fluke Wish-Wash hadn't put a foot in Gough's water bowl. Oodles swung around. "Anyway, I have no idea at all what you are talking about."

"Don't tell me you've forgotten about the DNA test already?"

Oodles tightened the cord of his green tartan dressing gown. "Of course I haven't forgotten. What are you implying?"

"If your short-term memory was any flamin' good you'd recall that this trip was the prize they were offering for the winner." Wish-Wash took a small red folder from his pocket, and waved it. "An all-expenses trip for two to wherever you came from. Business-class."

"And you won! I'll be blowed." Oodles gazed vacantly out the kitchen window. "Do they know how old you are?"

"They've got my DNA, haven't they?"

"You muppet. DNA won't tell them your age!"

"You don't know that? If the testing is smart enough to tell them my ancestors came from Donegal, don't you think they'd be able to work out my age?"

"From a scraping of gob from inside your cheek? You reckon they'd be able to place you in the Jurassic period, do you?"

"You can laugh! You're too scared to use a computer but now you think you know everything there is to know about science!"

"Gawdsake! Don't get me started on the computer again. I'm *not* afraid of technology. I just don't see why I need one." Oodles switched off the jug. "If Sally Hopkins says we need a computer at the museum, well, I'd be foolish arguing with someone like her who knows her way around the tourism industry. But you haven't come up with one good reason for me to have a computer here."

"You'd be able to email me."

"You could always walk up here."

"What if I needed you in a hurry?"

Oodles poured the hot water into the teapot and covered it with a red, white and blue woollen tea cosy.

"It's not just email," Wish-Wash said. "Think of the other things you could do with a computer?"

Oodles got a carton of milk out of the fridge and carried it to the table in the living room, with Wish-Wash trudging right behind him.

Oodles turned around, and put his hands on his hips. "You could at least have carried something, old son."

"I thought you'd want to hear about the trip."

"This is the first time I've known you to let something else come between you and a cuppa."

Oodles returned to the kitchen and came back with a laden wooden tray that he plonked on to the yellow formica table.

He transferred the teapot, the sugar bowl, a couple of teaspoons, a tea strainer, and two mugs. He sat down opposite Wish-Wash.

Oodles held out his palms. "Go on? Name one good reason why I need a computer at home?"

Wish-Wash scratched his prickly whiskers. "I dunno. I'm discovering new things every day . . . "

"One thing!"

"All right then. We could be friends on The Facebook."

"Are you kidding me!"

"How do you feel about Twitter?"

"Gawdsake! You haven't signed up to social media, have you?"

"Not yet. But even if I can't convince you I don't reckon finding friends would be difficult. Barely a day goes by I don't receive an email from a beautiful woman who says she wants to get to know me better."

Oodles rolled his eyes. "You don't reply, do you?"

"Of course not. I don't think Moose would want to give up his kingsize bed, do you? The flat is cramped enough with just two of us; adding an internet bride to the mix would be just asking for trouble." Wish-Wash made a point of looking around. "You, on the other hand, have two spare bedrooms. You could have your own harem."

Oodles held up his ring finger. "What don't you understand about *Until Death Do Us Part*? BOTH DEATHS!"

"You were the one who asked what you could do with a computer."

"Bad enough you're trying to knock my eyes out with that bright shirt, now you're asking me to divert much-needed blood from my heart!"

"You're going to need a computer to do research if you want to come on this trip with me." Wish-Wash jabbed an index finger at the folder, which was now on the table.

"I hate to disappoint you, old cock, but even if I wanted to go with you, my medical issues might make travel insurance prohibitively expensive."

Wish-Wash started laughing. *Hee-haw, hee-haw.* "You don't need to worry about that!" He tapped the folder again. "Read it for yourself. All expenses are paid, including the insurance."

"Gawdsake! I might not even get medical permission to fly all that way."

Wish-Wash's smile became even broader. "I've already sussed that out. I went to see Doc Jenkins yesterday."

"You didn't?"

"I've actually had these tickets for a week, but it took that long to get an appointment with the quack."

———

Oodles suspected James Northan would be peeved. "Have you told the Mayor yet?" he asked.

"I wanted to surprise him by sending him a postcard from Ireland. But I haven't seen the old sod. Have you?"

Now Oodles thought about it, they hadn't seen hide nor hair of James for more than a week. They had maintained an uneasy truce with him after mailing in the two DNA samples. He hadn't lowered himself to sitting on the bench with them but he had joined them for a few pots of tea, keeping up his barrage of odd language.

James's daughter Maddie was actually the mayor these days. But they'd normally see James poncing around town like he thought he should still be.

James's great, great, great grandfather, Colonel Richard Northan, had founded the town of Windy Mountain in 1841, and when James ascended to the mayoral chains, every mayor had come from that same bloodline.

Conversely, Wish-Wash was the first person in his family to become town drunk. But he forged a reputation as the best town drunk Windy Mountain had ever had.

That all came to an abrupt end though shortly after a wintry night in 1967.

Wish-Wash had been napping in the bus shelter in the High Street when he was woken up by a growling noise around 3am.

He claimed that when he glanced up, a Tasmanian Tiger was gawking down at him.

The problem with this story was that the last Tasmanian Tiger in captivity had died in 1936, so the likelihood of the shy marsupial dog making a comeback in the Windy Mountain main street in the swinging sixties was quite unlikely.

But the media still milked the story for all it was worth.

James, who really was the mayor back then, claimed, however, Wish-Wash had made the town the butt of jokes, and took steps to make sure his claim could never be verified. He also lobbied to have him sacked as town drunk.

This is how the big man lost the only job he had ever aspired to.

Wish-Wash had served for 13 stellar years and his name had been the most revered on the town drunk honour board which hung in The Applecart pub. A long line of people had since tried and failed to maintain his high standards. The latest incumbent in the job was Barely Legal Leigh.

When Father O'Boring (real name Father John O'Rourke) finally met his maker in the church fire 18 months ago at age 92, it left Wish-Wash, James and Oodles as the last three old blokes in town.

———

Oodles stroked the tea cosy. Madge had knitted that from soft wool she had brought back from England. Now she was gone, it would feel funny getting on a plane without her. "So what did Doc Jenkins say?"

Wish-Wash straightened in his chair. "He gave me a green light. He said nothing was wrong with me. He didn't exactly say so, but I reckon now I've worked out how to use the cash register at the museum and

I've mastered the new computer he'd be fine with me actually flying the plane."

Oodles rolled his eyes. "But me? What did he say about me?"

Wish-Wash surveyed the things laid out on the table. "I knew something was missing? You've forgotten the biscuits again!"

"Never mind that. What did Jenko say about me?"

"Shall I be mother?" Wish-Wash picked up the teapot and poured tea into the two mugs.

Glug, glug, glug.

"What are you holding back?" Oodles said.

"Nothing. I'm just waiting for the bickies."

Oodles got up wearily and went to the cupboard in the kitchen. He came back and threw an unopened packet of Iced Vo-Vo's on to the table.

Wish-Wash's eyes lit up. "Ooh la la, very fancy."

"Now will you tell me what he said?" Oodles sat down again.

"As I said, Doc Jenkins gave me the green light. But I'm afraid he's only given you the amber light."

Wish-Wash ripped open the packet, examined the biscuits to make sure they were all the same size, made his choice, dunked it into his steaming cup, then sucked on it noisily before stuffing the soggy biscuit into his mouth. He pulled a face, as if he had just sucked on a lemon. "Why didn't you remind me I hadn't put sugar in my tea?"

"Gawdsake! As if those biscuits aren't sweet enough! But never mind what you're doing to your teeth. Can I travel or not?"

Wish-Wash answered with a shower of crumbs. "You can travel but only if someone accompanies you."

Oodles lifted his mug towards his lips, surreptitiously also watching Wish-Wash spoon four teaspoons of sugar into his tea. "What are you saying?"

Wish-Wash stirred noisily. By the look of it, he was also combing his mouth with his tongue searching for pockets of biscuits. Then came the little sucking noises.

When he was satisfied he had got them all, Wish-Wash looked Oodles in the eye. "Doc Jenkins wants me to go as your carer."

————

"Carer!" It was lucky Oodles had just swallowed a mouthful of tea otherwise he'd look like a fire hose. "Be buggered if I'm going to let you nursemaid me."

"It's because you're Ukrainian, isn't it?"

"What?" Oodles wiped his lips with a hand. "Who said I'm Ukrainian?"

"You did. All those months ago. It's why you didn't want to take the DNA test. You said you couldn't care less if you were Ukrainian, or not."

"That was just an example. I might well have Latvian forebears as far as I know."

"Same difference. It helps to explain your independent streak."

Oodles wondered if Wish-Wash even knew where Ukraine or Latvia were on the map, let alone know anything about their qualities of independent spirit. He held him in his gaze.

"Don't look at me like that? Admit it. You'll need me on this trip."

"Need you? You're assuming I'll even agree to go with you."

"Why wouldn't you?" Wish-Wash said. "This will be the trip of a lifetime."

"More likely it will be the trip that ends our lives."

"What do you mean?"

"Don't you watch the news?" Oodles said. "Plane crashes, terrorists, bubonic plague–"

"Donegal doesn't have any flamin' bubonic plague. All they've had is the potato famine."

Oodles took another swig of his tea, then he pushed the packet of biscuits towards Wish-Wash. "Here, have another one. I'm all out of your pills."

Wish-Wash's hand was halfway to the packet before he reacted. "Oh, very funny! You forget green light here doesn't take any pills. One of my jobs on the trip will be to make sure amber light takes all his."

He extracted another Iced Vo-Vo and examined it like a long lost friend. "But thanks for the thought." He dunked it into his cup, then sucked it into his mouth. It was like watching a whale gulping pink plankton.

Oodles tutted. "At this rate, the plane won't even be able to get off the ground because of the weight."

Wish-Wash placed his index fingers into his ears, and sprayed more crumbs over the table. "I can't hear a word you're saying."

"Oh, don't be so childish! I bet you don't even know where Donegal is."

Wish-Wash swallowed. "Do too! I've been doing research on the computer."

"So where is it, then?"

"North-west Ireland."

"You have been busy. Doing any work?"

Wish-Wash wriggled in his chair. "We had four tour groups through yesterday. V did more than 100 teas and coffees."

"You helped her then?"

"What do you think I am? Mandrake?"

————

Oodles herded Wish-Wash towards the front door.

"What's the hurry?"

"I thought you said you were busy at the museum?"

Wish-Wash stepped down the three steps into the empty carport, and Oodles nearly ran into the back of him. "The first tour group won't arrive until 9am, which means I had plenty of time to finish that packet of biscuits for you."

"I thought you preferred chocolate digestives."

"I do. You can't dunk Iced Vo-Vo's in your tea properly."

"That didn't seem to stop you!"

"You should have seen the pink goop in the bottom of my cup."

Oodles blinked slowly, but the vision was painted on the insides of his eyelids — giving him something to look forward to when he came to wash the dishes.

Wish-Wash picked at the shoulder of Oodles's woollen dressing gown. "Anyone would think it's the middle of winter!"

Oodles slapped his hand away. "Do you mind? Madge bought me this."

"Did she also buy you a set of bagpipes? Maybe your ancestors came from Scotland?"

"Will you lay off. I told you I don't give a damn where I come from." Oodles said.

"I just hope that daggy old dressing gown stays here when we go to Ireland."

"You know the Irish also have tartans? Didn't your computer tell you that? Why don't you put that in your pipe and smoke it?"

Wish-Wash reached into his coat pocket and pulled out his packet of cigarettes, probably to emphasise he didn't actually smoke a pipe. That was Oodles's caper. Or it used to be. Doc Jenkins had been on at him for years to give it up for the sake of his health. The doctor finally stopped nagging, and that's when Oodles had quit just to show he could. Now he watched as Wish-Wash popped a fag into his mouth.

"How are you going to stand going without a smoke during that long flight?" Oodles said.

Wish-Wash's eyes popped. "They won't let me smoke? Even in business class?"

"Not even if they *do* let you fly the plane." Oodles smiled. "You'll have to go cold turkey all that way."

"I don't know what you find so funny?" Wish-Wash said. "It won't be much fun for you, either, cobber, having the passenger next to you sweating like a pig, and tossing and turning when you're trying to get some kip."

"You haven't been listening to me! I'm no certainty to even be on that plane with you. It's easier for you. You don't answer to anybody. For a start, who's going to take care of the dog if I go away?"

Wish-Wash shrugged. "Any one of a number of people. Moose, Joffa, Katy, Tim . . . "

Oodles glared at him. "Tim? Who the heck is Tim?"

Wish-Wash smacked his forehead. "I knew I had something else I needed to tell you. I forgot all about it because of the excitement over our trip."

"You still don't get it. I'll need to think it over."

"Take all the time you need. We've still got four weeks."

"Four weeks! Strewth!"

"I don't know what's wrong with you? All you have to do is sit back and enjoy being pampered. If Tim can travel halfway around the world at his age . . . "

"There you go again! Who is this blinking Tim?"

The unlit durry in Wish-Wash's mouth bobbed up and down, but his voice just went up. "If you would just listen, I'm trying to tell you." He let that admonishment sit for a moment, then said, "He starts work at the museum this morning."

"We can't afford another employee!"

"We can actually. Have you checked our bank account lately?"

"How much are we paying him?"

Wish-Wash coughed into his hand. "I didn't say we were paying him. He's one of them interns. You remember that rich Yank who came to town years ago?"

Oodles stared into space. "Yes," he finally said. "Big bloke who looked like Rupert Bear wearing a stetson hat?"

"Tim is his grandson. He calls himself Tim Noah the Fourth. Speaks just like the old bloke too. His voice goes up and down like a yo-yo."

"Why's he here? You don't think his grandfather is making another attempt to buy us out, do you?"

Wish-Wash shrugged.

He was holding his unlit cigarette between fat fingers on his right hand, and he folded his arms. "Apparently, he's chosen Windy Mountain as one of his stops on his way to see the world, and he's agreed to work for us for nothing."

"Really? It won't cost us a cent?"

Wish-Wash coughed into his hand again. "I didn't say that either. We're paying for his board at The Applecart."

The pub let out a few cheap, shabby rooms upstairs. Wish-Wash even used to have a room there before he moved to the museum. His hotel room wasn't much bigger than a shoebox, had a black and white TV that only sometimes worked, and he had to share a bathroom with five other residents.

"You should be happy he seems so capable because now I can meet you up at the Wind Tunnel Cafe around 11 o'clock," Wish-Wash said.

"You're leaving him in charge? Strewth! Didn't you say it's his first day!"

"So? He has to learn sometime. I haven't had a break for days."

He popped the fag back in his mouth and took a match out of its box.

"Don't you dare light up here!"

"Why not?" Wish-Wash looked around at the empty carport. "I presume your pride and joy is safely parked in the garage, where I can't flick ash on it?"

"It is. But I don't want smoke wafting back in the house."

"Why not? It'd make the place smell better."

"My house doesn't smell!"

"It smells of old man, bleach and mothballs."

"You know I didn't lay any of those mothballs. When I find them, I turf them out. It's not my fault Madge scattered them around like a treasure hunt."

"What are you doing about the old man smell?"

Oodles glared at him. "I suppose your place smells of roses?"

"Cigarette smoke, actually. I'm offering you my deodorising service. But if you don't want it, can't you just close the flamin' door?"

"No, I blinking can't. I don't want to accidentally lock myself out in my dressing gown."

"Typical!" Wish-Wash pointed to the sky. "No clouds. It's going to be a beautiful summer's day and you're dressed like McScott of the Antarctic."

THREE
IT'S MY LADDER AND I'LL PRY IF I WANT TO

OODLES WATCHED Wish-Wash disappear down the hill beneath plumes of cigarette smoke, then he went back inside.

He came out of the back door 10 minutes later fully dressed, and carrying a leash and a dog poop bag.

He ought to have been wearing shorts on a nice morning like today, but he was a creature of habit dressed in his faded overalls.

At least his white floppy towelling hat provided some shade.

Gough started barking and rattling his chain.

The dog belonged to the museum but the services he once provided weren't required any more so he had gone to live with Oodles.

"Hello boy. Ready for walkies?" Oodles scratched behind Gough's ears.

The grey-muzzled pooch had to be 15 or 16.

Heaven knows what kind of dog he was. Oodles and Wish-Wash had hoped to find a doppelgänger for James's miniature collie but they had struck out when they went shopping at the RSPCA in Launceston. Gough was the right height but his head was too big and his tail was all wrong. God might well have designed him using one of those mix-

and-match flick card-sets. *This* head on *that* body with *that* tail and *these* legs.

Oodles undid the chain and attached the lead.

They always walked down to the High Street, where Oodles allowed Gough to cock his leg on the imposing bronze statue in the middle of the street. When Oodles had worked as the council works supervisor he had lost count of how many times James Northan had instructed him to get a ladder and wipe the bird poop from his great, great, great grandfather's hat. So letting the dog now do his business on Colonel Northan's horse's hind legs gave him a sense of revenge.

After the statue, Oodles and Gough would continue across the road — straight through the wrought iron gate into the Colonel Richard Northan Memorial Rose Garden, so Gough could dig some holes in the hallowed ground.

Many of the flowers from the garden ended up on Billy Gumboots's grave, which was a source of exasperation for the Mayor.

James couldn't prove Wish-Wash raided the park when it was dark.

No one ever saw Wish-Wash at the cemetery either.

But every morning his son's grave was usually the most colourful and fragrant in the graveyard.

After the park, Oodles and Gough headed back through the gate to the High Street and walked up to the Tasmanian Tiger Museum.

He doffed his floppy hat to Wish-Wash through the big windows of the museum, and crossed the road to the decrepit Colonel Richard Northan Memorial Park Bench.

He had painted that bench green many times when he worked on the council, and in retirement had spent many hours sitting there whiling away the time with Wish-Wash and sometimes James.

Oodles bent down and looked Gough in the eye. "If Madge says it's all right, what would you say if I went away on a little holiday with Wish-Wash, and you went to stay with someone?"

———

Oodles was leaning against the side wall when Wish-Wash approached the cafe.

"Why didn't you go in out of the sun?" Wish-Wash said. "I might have been a while showing the cocky American kid the ropes?"

Oodles rubbed the side of his sweaty neck. "You know I still feel awkward when I am alone with Wendy."

"Why? We didn't have anything to do with putting Gordo away."

Oodles removed his hat as they passed through the door.

Wendy was wiping down a table, but she glanced up as the bead curtains rustled. "Have you had a falling out with the Mayor again?"

"No," Wish-Wash said. "We haven't seen him around for a week." He turned to Oodles. "Have we?"

The old men dragged back their chairs and sat down. "How is Gordo, Wendy?" Wish-Wash asked.

"He'd be a lot better if he wasn't sharing a cell with Freddy Cuthbert. That's what you get for your taxes!" Wendy rolled her eyes. "That dropkick got him into trouble in the first place!"

Wendy resumed wiping, and when she was happy with her work, stood up straight and put her hands on her hips, and sighed. "What can I get you both?"

"The usual."

She met Wish-Wash's gaze. "Three cups and a plate of biscuits, love?"

Wish-Wash considered this. "We only need two cups but we'll have the same number of biscuits. Jimbo would want me to have his."

"So, any ideas where he is?"

Wish-Wash shook his head. "Maybe he's down in Hobart visiting your hubby in Risdon Prison?" The comment brought him glares from both sides.

Wendy turned without speaking and disappeared through the swinging doors into the kitchen.

"Why did you have to say that?" Oodles said.

"I'm allowed to speculate, aren't I? Or perhaps he's visiting Freddy?"

"Gawdsake! James used to cross the High Street if he saw Freddy coming his way."

"That doesn't mean anything. Jimbo does the same whenever he sees Moose coming his way, Heck, us too. And a lot of people cross the road when they see *him* coming."

"Will you cut it out?" Oodles changed the subject. "So if this lad Tim is looking after the museum, where are Moose and Joffa?"

"They've gone bush. I thought they'd be back yesterday, but I haven't even heard from them on the CB."

"Perhaps they are out of radio range?"

"They don't normally stay out this long." Wish-Wash sighed. "I suppose I should be thankful *Wonder-boy* turned up to help us out."

"Why do I get the sense he's already getting on your wick?"

"You should hear him?" Wish-Wash looked up towards the ceiling. "Everything is *awesome sauce* this or *awesome sauce* that. It's like I have to learn another language. And another thing: I've been learning the ins and outs of that flamin' computer for a week now and he has the cheek to tell me I'm not using it to a fraction of its potential."

"Can you blame him? He probably grew up with computers, so it's probably excruciating to him watching you typing with one finger."

"Very funny. I'm now using both my index fingers, if you must know. But it's not just the computer. He shooed me away when I offered to show him how to operate the cash register — like I was an old fuddy-duddy."

"I hate to say it, but you *are* an old fuddy-duddy."

"Careful. Who's caring for who on this trip to Ireland?"

"I haven't even agreed to go with you yet." Oodles shrugged. "But you shouldn't lose sleep over a kid who's still wet around the ears. I'd think you'd know more about Tasmanian Tigers than him."

Wish-Wash's eyes lit up. "Yeah, I didn't get round to telling him I've actually seen one. But I will. Bloody oath I will. That'll give him something to make his sauce really flamin' awesome."

They both raised their heads when Wendy backed through the swinging door with a tray.

They turned again when someone came swishing through the bead curtains over the front door.

It was Norm Hit, the new editor and sole full-time employee of *The Pick of the Crop* online newspaper.

Norm had an uneasy history with James.

They had first locked horns in the early 1990s when James was the mayor and Norm was in his eyes a troublesome cadet journalist.

To James's horror, Norm went on to book a place in the Northan family by marrying Maddie. When they adopted Korean twins Vicki and Velda, James was beside himself. How dare they pollute the bloodline! It got worse. The now-teenage girls were now working in catering at the Tasmanian Tiger Museum. Few people could tell them apart, so they were just known as the Vs.

Norm met Wish-Wash's eyes as Wendy laid down the tray. "Better fetch another cup, after all," Wish-Wash said to the waitress.

Norm raised a hand. "Not for me, thanks, Wish-Wash. I've just popped in for a takeaway. Someone's nicked the population signs at either end of the town."

Oodles tutted. It had always worried him when he worked on the council the sign at one end said the population of the town was 3003, and the other end said it had 3004 citizens, but he was never allowed to fix them because he was told by his bosses that's the way they had always been and it wasn't worth upsetting people by imposing changes on them.

"Sergeant Stretch is bewildered," Norm said. "He says he can understand how signs get vandalised, but why would anyone just nick them?"

"What does Maddie say?" Oodles said.

Norm shrugged. "She's been at one of those hush-hush municipal meetings. She wasn't even allowed to tell me where it is being held."

"So that's where James must be too?" Oodles said.

"She never said," Norm said.

"Really?" Oodles squinted. "You must know he hasn't been around for a week?"

"Why would I? Since he put his dog down, we hardly hear a peep from the granny flat. He hasn't come near me since I went back to *The Pick of the Crop*."

Norm watched Wendy making his instant coffee. "His bedroom light is on every time I look."

Oodles poured the tea. "Have you got a key to the place?"

"Somewhere, but don't ask me where it is. Maddie is out of phone contact wherever she is. She'll be back at the weekend though."

Oodles rattled his saucer as he picked up his cup. "You wouldn't mind if Wish-Wash and I had a shufty through the windows? I'd hate to think he was sick or injured."

———

"I dunno if I have time." Wish-Wash was carrying the front end of the ladder along the footpath, and had to turn his head to talk to Oodles who was carrying the back end. "*Wonder-boy* might need my help back at the museum."

"Will you watch where you're going! The last thing we want is to scrape the side of one of these parked cars."

"You heard Norm. Jimbo hardly speaks to him. He's probably just gone away for a bit and not told him."

Oodles put his end of the ladder down, dragging Wish-Wash to a standstill too. "I can't imagine James going away without big-noting he's flying first-class to Paris or somewhere, can you?"

"First time for everything." Wish-Wash shook his hands. "He might just have keeled over."

"How can you even think such a thing?"

"What goes around, comes around. Do you think he gave a rat's arse about sending Howard to doggie heaven?"

Oodles gazed into the middle distance. Wish-Wash had a point. Poor Howard hadn't even reached his time. As soon as the ban was lifted prohibiting people who weren't mayors or ex-mayors from owning dogs in Windy Mountain, James had ordered for his miniature collie to be euthanised. He justified this by saying his pure-bred dog wouldn't be seen dead with common dogs like Gough.

Wish-Wash snapped Oodles back to the present. "I haven't got all day, you know?"

"What?"

"Standing here on the footpath isn't getting this ladder anywhere." He reached into his pocket for a handkerchief, which he used to mop his brow. "Pity Moose and Joffa weren't here. They'd both be tall enough not to need a ladder to look in all those windows."

"This won't wait. James could be lying on the floor unconscious."

"We all have to go sometime."

"Wish-Wash!" Oodles glared at him.

"Have you forgotten he tried to diddle us out of thousands of dollars?"

"You forget that whole thing gave us the money to buy the museum," Oodles said. "It was James who lost his life savings."

"Oh, my heart bleeds for him. The poor old fellow has nothing now."

Oodles knew Wish-Wash was being sarcastic. James still lived in his designer flat in the lush grounds of his daughter's estate. Technically, he had nothing but the government pension to tide him over. But Maddie probably compensated him with the odd dollar or a thousand. The Northans had always eaten from the same taxpayer-funded gilded pig trough.

"Let's get going again." Oodles raised his end of the ladder. "Otherwise we'll never get there."

Wish-Wash pressed his nose up against the bedroom window. "He hasn't closed the curtains. Looks like he's made his bed."

Oodles looked across from the window on the other side of the verandah. "What do you make of that?"

Wish-Wash shrugged. "That he's more anal-retentive than we even thought?"

"What's wrong with making your bed each day?"

"Why would you make your bed when you're only going to mess it up again when you get in it?"

Oodles shook his head. "Some carer you're going to be!"

"Doesn't mean I'll have to make your bed."

"Are you sure?" Oodles trotted down the steps and headed towards the ladder they had rested sideways against an oak tree. "Read the fine print, have you?"

Wish-Wash followed him. "I thought you hadn't even made up your mind you were coming?"

Oodles turned. "I'm still weighing up the pros and cons, and I need to clear it with Madge."

"Madge! You've found a way to talk to the dead, have you?"

"Don't be disrespectful!" Oodles glared at him. "I bet you talk to Billy at his grave?"

"Maybe. But he never answers!"

"Madge and I were together for a lot longer than you two were. It got that way we didn't always have to speak to know what the other was thinking."

"That'll add a new dimension when you're doing your seance. I didn't even know you had a Luigi board."

"That would be an Ouija board, you muppet. But for your information, I don't need one. Madge visits me in my dreams. I don't think she'd be too impressed at the prospect of me sharing a room with a carer who doesn't make his bed and refuses to make mine?"

Wish-Wash scowled. "If I was you and Madge, I'd be more worried about what that kid might be doing at the museum right now."

"You hired him. And you were the one who let him fly solo."

"I didn't know I'd be gone so long though. That's down to you."

"Oh no, you can't put the blame on me." Oodles waved an index finger. "I didn't ask the Mayor to disappear." Oodles picked up his end of the ladder and nodded for Wish-Wash to do the same. "We're only doing what we'd hope he'd do for us."

"You don't really think he'd give a toss about us?"

Oodles started backing up towards the side of the granny flat. "Probably not. But I'd never forgive myself if he's lying crook on the floor."

They placed the ladder against the brick wall.

The ladder went way past the roofline. But the rhododendron bushes still made the windows difficult to get at.

"Are you going up, or me?" Wish-Wash said.

Oodles gave him a searing look because they both knew Wish-Wash had terrible balance.

"What?"

"Don't pretend you're volunteering!"

"I'm not. But I've followed your orders so far, haven't I? I might point out you're the one who wants to be the knight in shining armour, cobber. What did you see in the other front room anyway?"

"Not much," Oodles said. "Nothing to see but some chesterfield sofas and a coffee table."

"Did Jimbo ever invite you to have coffee with him in there?"

"You know he didn't. I never got past the front door, just like you."

"What does that tell you? We've never been good enough for him." Wish-Wash swept his arm over the vista. Lawns manicured like bowling greens, mighty oak trees that probably were sown at the time the town was established, colourful flower beds and espaliered fruit trees. "I wouldn't mind being this poor."

Oodles began climbing the ladder. "Just hold it steady, will you? We need to look in all these windows — otherwise neither of us will be able to sleep tonight."

The ladder creaked and groaned as Oodles climbed and came face-to-face with the glass.

"What can you see?" Wish-Wash said.

Oodles put his forehead against the window.

"It looks like the kitchen." Oodles squinted to see past the glare. "Yes, it is. I can see the stove . . . and the sink . . . I can see a notepad on the server."

Wish-Wash suddenly sounded chirpy. "You don't think he's left a suicide note?"

"James top himself?" Oodles gasped. "I doubt it."

"What's the note say?"

"I can't read it from here, can I!"

"Why did you have to go and get my hopes up, then?"

Oodles began backing down the ladder.

When he got to the bottom, Wish-Wash was flicking a lighter at the cigarette bobbing in his mouth.

"You'd better hope James is *not* inside," Oodles said. "He'd have a fit if he sees you smoking in his garden."

"Do I look scared?"

"C'mon." Oodles took hold of the ladder. "Let's move it to the next window."

———

The old men carried the ladder back up the hill, backed it into the garage and hung it on the hooks on the wall — careful not to scratch Oodles's ute.

"I'd better get back," Wish-Wash said. "Last thing I want is for that Yank kid to raise a posse to come find me."

"What do you think this is? A blinking cowboy movie?"

Wish-Wash looked him in the eye, well as much as you could in the murky light of a garage with a low-watt globe. "You haven't seen him!"

"I reckon you would have told me if he had turned up wearing a Stetson hat."

"He was wearing a *black* baseball cap on *backwards*. What do you make of that?"

Oodles shook his head. "Where's he tied up his horse? Guess I'll soon see. I have to come back to the museum with you. I need to use the phone to call Norm so I can tell him what we saw in the kitchen."

"What's wrong with your land-line phone?"

"I got it cut off. It was a waste of money. I don't call any bugger, and the only people who'd call me were Indian scammers telling me they needed to take remote control of my computer so they could fix it."

Wish-Wash squinted. "For crying out loud, how am I going to rouse you now if I need you?"

"The exercise will do you good. Or if you really don't want to walk, try emailing me."

Oodles slapped his forehead in mock realisation. "I forgot. I don't have a computer, do I? I guess that's why I gave the scammers your number. You've got something they can actually fix."

———

Oodles extended a hand. Tim Noah was 18 or 19, tall and skinny with glasses but the family resemblance only kicked in when he started talking in his Texan twang.

"You met my granddaddy?" The kid adjusted his glasses with his other hand. "He drives us mad talking about the day he attended that crazy football match."

Oodles looked around at Wish-Wash. "I had forgotten Tim's grandfather went to the grand final. It was the year Billy Gumboots lost us the game . . . "

As soon as he said it, he regretted saying it.

Wish-Wash gave him a dirty look. "You have to forgive Oodles here, Timbo. He'll be out of our hair soon because he's only come by to use the phone. For a silent partner, he has a lot to say."

Noah looked confused. "Granddaddy could never work out why one dude on the whole park had to wear gumboots."

"It's a long story," Oodles said. "When you meet Moose, maybe he'll explain it."

"The Moose?" Noah spoke excitedly. "He's still around?"

Oodles turned to Wish-Wash. "Didn't you tell him?"

"When have I had the flamin' chance to tell him anything? I was looking in windows with you half the morning." Wish-Wash stabbed his thumb towards Oodles. "I haven't even had time to tell Tim I'm taking you to Ireland? *As your carer.*"

The Texan's face took on a red tinge as he stumbled over his words, and pointed back to the computer. "Mr Whish-Willson did spend a lot of the morning explaining how that works."

Oodles stared blankly. "What did you call him?"

Noah fumbled with his words. "My pappy always taught me to respect my elders."

"Gawdsake!" Oodles exhaled deeply. "Even his mother used to call him by his nickname. He's Wish-Wash, I'm Oodles. Moose and Joffa do the actual tracking of the Tasmanian Tigers. Nobody goes by their given names around here! Don't worry, we'll think of a nickname for *you* too."

Noah walked behind the desk and turned the monitor their way. "I could never have built this without his help."

The computer screen showed a flashing screensaver that announced the name of the museum and featured a large picture of a Tasmanian Tiger. "Awesome sauce, eh? What do you think?" Tim said.

"You're trying to tell me he helped you with that!" Oodles suppressed a coughing fit.

The Texan sat down on the high stool behind the counter. "So when will I meet Moose? Granddaddy said he was a big, angry dude . . ."

"Joffa is just as big," Wish-Wash blurted. "You'd be forgiven for thinking they were brothers."

"Until you hear them speak," Oodles said. "Joffa comes from Ireland."

———

The call to Norm lasted about 10 minutes.

Oodles had barely put the receiver down when Wish-Wash asked, "What did he say?"

"Same as before. He says he doesn't know where the key is. We'll have to wait until Maddie gets home."

"Did you tell him about the note?"

"You didn't hear me say?"

"I'm not an earwig." He turned to the American. "We were talking, weren't we?"

Tim nodded.

"Norm didn't seem too fussed," Oodles said. "He said it was probably one of James's poems."

"What poems?"

Oodles shrugged. "News to me too."

"He never told us he was writing poetry." Wish-Wash wrinkled his nose.

"Love sonnets, apparently. Norm says James has it in his head he might be able to trace his lineage back to William Shakespeare."

"Typical Jimbo," Wish-Wash said.

"It explains why he started talking funny," Oodles said. "Still can't get Moose and Joffa on the radio?"

Wish-Wash shook his head. "Here you go again! When have I had the flamin' chance?"

"When I was on the phone perhaps?"

Wish-Wash shrugged. "It's not like them to be incommunicado. Funny Katy hasn't called to find out where they are?"

The Texan cleared his throat. "Actually I think she did. While you were out Mr . . . er, Wish-Wash."

"Katy is Joffa's wife," Oodles explained.

"That makes sense now. But it didn't at the time. I assumed it was Wish-Wash's wife. She wanted to know why her husband hadn't been home for three nights. My first thought was Wish-Wash was having a little o' thang on the side. But my mind went blank, so I just hung up."

Oodles pinched the bridge of his nose. "Couldn't you tell by the sound of her voice Katy's about 50 years younger than Wish-Wash?" He pointed to his partner. "Wish-Wash hasn't even got an *old* wife. Do you think Katy'd have anything to do with an old fart like him?"

FOUR
LEAN ON ME
TUESDAY MORNING

WISH-WASH FLUNG OPEN the front door of the museum with enough force to test the strength of the hinges.

"You missed all the flamin' drama," he called out.

Oodles swung around. "What drama?"

"It looks like Moose might have busted his leg."

Oodles finished tying Gough to a post at the edge of the footpath. He had been trying to work out what he was going to say to Wish-Wash as the little dog towed him ever closer towards the museum. Now, it seemed, he could put it off for a bit longer.

He stepped past Wish-Wash, who was holding the door open.

"When did they get back?" Oodles asked.

"A couple of hours ago." Wish-Wash followed him across the foyer. "Moose hobbled in with his arm across Joffa's shoulder."

Oodles turned and faced him. "How far had they come like that?"

"Miles."

Oodles winced. "That must have hurt." He looked left and right. "So where is everyone?"

"Joffa took Moose to the hospital, and I sent *Wonder-boy* with them to help. With any luck, he won't remember how to get home."

"That's a terrible thing to say."

"Fair dinkum! If he shows me one more fancy thing on that computer . . . "

"I thought you liked the computer."

"The novelty is wearing off. And don't get me started on the doorbell."

"Is it broken again?"

Oodles didn't think it was possible Wish-Wash could screw up his face any further, but he was wrong. "No, *Wonder-boy* disengaged it on my orders. Good thing too. The new chimes would have been the final straw for Moose after making it all the way home in that state."

Oodles searched Wish-Wash's eyes for further explanation, but nothing was offered.

The time had arrived for him to bite the bullet. "Cheer up. I've got some good news for you. I talked to Madge last night, and she's fine with me going on the trip. So, I've decided 99 per cent I will go to Ireland with you."

"Really?" Wish-Wash looked like he was about to start jumping up and down like an excited toddler.

Oodles threw out a palm. "But I still need the all-clear from Doc Jenkins."

Wish-Wash's face darkened. "Didn't you hear a word I said? Jenko's already given you the amber light. Isn't my word good enough for you?"

"I want to hear it from the organ grinder, not the monkey."

"That's a nice thing to say! I can't believe you want to give Doc Jenkins a chance to change his mind. What if he now says no?"

"That's obvious. I won't be going if that's the case."

———

Gus Foot and Joffa were sitting on either side of Moose's bed when Wish-Wash and Oodles walked into the hospital room.

Gus got to his feet and held out his hand. "Oodles, Wishy, long time no see. Recognise this room?"

It was like the early 90s all over again. Only this time it was Moose dressed in a white hospital gown with bandages around his ankle. Back then, it was Gus. In those days, however, he went by the bikie name of Foetus. But he had reinvented himself. These days, he was an investment adviser, who drove a BMW sports car, cultivated an impressive beer gut and kept his shirt sleeves rolled down so no one could see his tattoos.

Wish-Wash brightened up the room's beige colour-scheme with his green shirt, slightly different shade of green trousers and loosened red tie. He also carried a bunch of yellow roses.

Oodles's eyes locked on to Moose's. "What happened?"

"I tripped over a damn fallen tree."

"I thought you knew where all the dead trees were on the mountain?"

"Not that deep into the bush." Moose glanced up at the bleary-eyed Joffa. "We were tracking an animal for two days and followed it to the other side of Bing Bong Mountain."

"A Tiger? Are you sure?"

Moose glanced down to his ankle and laughed. "I'd hate to think I went through all this pain in pursuit of a wallaby."

Everyone else laughed, except Joffa, who looked like he was having trouble keeping his eyes open and his head upright. Wish-Wash collected two red plastic chairs from the far side of the other bed, which was neatly made up waiting for the next patient, and put one on either side of Moose's bed.

Oodles slumped into his chair. "So, what's the damage?"

"They won't know until the swelling has gone down," Moose said. "The doctor said I should have put ice on it straight away, but where was I going to get ice from up there?"

"You could have gone without your scotch," Gus said.

Moose gave him a dark stare then looked back at Oodles. "So whether it's broken or badly sprained I won't know until tomorrow.

Whatever the verdict, it's going to put me out of action for a while so you're going to be stuck with me at base." He shook his head. "Pity. We had nearly caught up with that animal. I wanted to see the embarrassed look on James Northan's face when we came back with a cage holding a real live Tasmanian Tiger."

"Wouldn't have done you no good," Wish-Wash said. "The Mayor has gone missing."

Oodles nodded. "No one has seen him for about a week."

"He didn't go with you, Moose, did he?" Wish-Wash said.

Moose rubbed his neck. "Do you think I'd be lying here if he had? I would have made sure he tripped over that fucking tree first."

Oodles shifted in his chair. "Maddie's away, and Norm can't find the key to get into his house but Wish-Wash and me had a squizzy through his windows yesterday and couldn't see a sign of him."

"All we saw was his suicide note," Wish-Wash said.

"Strewth! We don't know that," Oodles said. "We couldn't read the writing from outside the window, so it might say anything."

"Norm thinks it might be one of his poems," Wish-Wash said.

Moose scratched his head. "I didn't know Norm wrote poems?"

"Not Norm," Wish-Wash said. "Jimbo. He's got it in his head he's descended from William Shakespeare."

Moose shook his head rapidly from side to side. "These drugs they've given me are stronger than I thought. I thought you just said the Mayor thinks he's related to Shakespeare."

"I did," Wish-Wash said.

"Makes sense when you think about it." Gus Foot reached out to give Moose a high-five. "Jimbo is always shaking when he sees you. Get it?"

Wish-Wash joined in the mirth. "Just when you thought Jimbo couldn't get more obnoxious, he's gone from bard to worse."

Oodles folded his arms. "Will you jokers knock it off? One theory is he might have gone off for a few days to write his poetry."

"I like Wish-Wash's suicide theory better." Moose gave Gus a return high-five.

Oodles looked from Gus to Moose. "This is serious." He looked at Wish-Wash across the bed. "Isn't it?"

"Personally, I think the No. 1 item of news is our impending trip to Ireland."

Moose gave Oodles a quizzical look, but before the old man could answer Wish-Wash was stabbing his thumb across the bed. "I'm going as his carer."

Oodles let out a hard sigh and closed his eyes. "Don't believe a word he says. Since *he's* never even been on a plane, I know who'll be looking after who."

"I won the tickets for doing the DNA test," Wish-Wash said. "Turns out my ancestors came from County Donegal."

Moose studied Oodles's face. "Did you also do the test?"

"Why do I need to know any of that nonsense?" Oodles said. "The whole thing was James's idea and the only disciple he recruited was Wish-Wash."

Wish-Wash beamed. "The Mayor didn't give a hoot about the holiday-for-two prize. He said no one ever wins those things."

"It's a fecking long way to fly in economy class." Until now, the only sounds that had come from Joffa were yawns but talk of going back to Ireland must have roused him. "Have you thought about the prospect of spending tenty-four hours sitting in a seat next to someone you don't care for?"

"Oh, Oodles isn't *that* bad," Wish-Wash said. "But who said anything about economy, anyway?" He rose from his chair. "This is business-class both ways. I half-hope Jimbo does turn up again so I can remind him about that."

Oodles shook his head again, slowly this time. "I just can't imagine him topping himself? I reckon he's gone along with Maddie on her trip and not told anyone. He hasn't been talking to Norm because he's gone back to the newspaper."

"Why would that worry him?" Joffa said.

"You missed all the fun not being here in 1994." Oodles closed his eyes to recall it all. "He never did like the newspaper. But he really hit the roof when they ran a front-page photo of Moose tying him to that tree."

"Best edition ever." Gus Foot gave Moose another high-five.

Oodles laughed. "While we're reminiscing, Moose, did you notice anything familiar about the kid who helped you to the hospital?"

"The Yank? Every time I wondered who the hell he was, the pain would kick in and hijack my train of thought."

"Didn't Wish-Wash tell you he's hired an intern?" Oodles said.

Moose looked like he was about to leap up in rage, even with his bandaged leg. "If you've hired him, what meaningful work will you have for me?"

Wish-Wash and Oodles exchanged looks.

Moose looked from face to face. "I have to do something to earn my keep? I don't know how long I'll be out of action."

"That's all I need!" Wish-Wash said. "*Two* blokes buggering up my computer!"

"Relax," Oodles said. "We'll find chores for you for however long you need. Won't we Wish-Wash? One thing you can do is keep an eye on Tim, try to work out if he's up to anything."

"Tim?" Moose said.

Oodles pinched his left eyebrow. "The intern. Tim Noah the Fourth to be precise."

"Noooo?" Moose rubbed the back of his neck.

"Yes. He's Tim Noah Junior's grandson."

"You think his family's making another attempt to buy us?"

"Can't be too careful," Wish-Wash said. "That's why it'd be good for you to keep an eye on *Wonder-boy*."

Moose smirked. "Is that what you call the kid?"

Oodles nodded. "If you ask me, it's a lousy nickname that he needs to rethink."

"Why?" Wish-Wash said.

"You can't keep calling him *Wonder-boy*. People will start thinking you're the head superhero! I don't know if the Slutz Plains op shop even sells capes, especially in your colours."

"Very funny. Have you got a better flamin' idea?"

"What about *Awesome Sauce*? That's gotta be more appropriate, don't you think?" He was meet with a knowing smile from Wish-Wash and puzzled looks from the others. "Give it time, fellas, I'm sure the penny will drop."

Moose turned to Gus. "Are you still doing business with his family?"

"I am indeed. It's a nice little money-spinner. Shame, Moose, you've got too much grey in your beard these days . . . " He looked over to Joffa. "But thank goodness for *your* regular contributions."

"Yeah, well, it's about time the big Irish git started paying his way." Moose glanced down at his ankle again. "Now I'm out of action, he's going to have to go bush solo for a while. Pity. I reckon we nearly had that Tiger."

"I could go with Joffa."

Four sets of eyes turned to Wish-Wash, who had risen from his chair again.

"Gawdsake!" Oodles said. "Just because you found the energy to leap out of your chair twice doesn't mean your old bones would withstand the rigours of traipsing around the bush."

"I'm younger than you!"

"I think you've already established that. Many, many times."

"Who's going to Ireland as whose carer?"

"Do you have to start banging on about that again?"

"Do you have a better idea? You heard Moose. We're nearly at the stage of catching a Tasmanian Tiger. That would knock a lot of smirks off a lot of faces."

———

Wendy was cleaning the table when Oodles swished through the bead curtains with Wish-Wash close behind.

"Look what the cat dragged in? I thought you blokes must have left me for a younger cafe."

Oodles planted himself on a chair. "No, you're stuck with us whether you like it or not, Wendy. Even if this town had another cafe, we just didn't feel like morning tea today. Moose is in hospital."

Wish-Wash sat down opposite and sucked in his stomach so Wendy had room to finish wiping the table-top.

She glanced up. "Oh, that is good news!"

"Good news?" Wish-Wash said. "Moose didn't have anything to do with Gordo going to jail!"

"That's debatable, love. Besides, you know as well as I do, Moose used to be a big wheel in Risdon Prison. Do you know how hard it is for Gordo to live up to that reputation?"

She lifted up her cloth, stood back and studied the table, then sighed. "So, what will it be?"

Oodles closed his eyes slowly. "Why do you always ask that? We haven't ordered anything different for about 30 years."

"That's not true. When there were seven or eight of you oldies, that meant more cups and a lot more biscuits."

"You really didn't have to reduce the biscuits," Wish-Wash said.

She gave him a dirty look. "Bad enough my hubby's in jail, now my best customers are dropping off the perch. Last week, you were down to three. Now you're two."

Oodles frowned. "Now hang on, we have no evidence James is dead."

Wendy stood with her hands on her hips. "Where is he then?"

"Norm thinks he might be on a trip writing poetry," Oodles said.

"Poetry?" She looked bemused. "The Mayor?"

"Our other theory is he's topped himself," Wish-Wash said.

Oodles looked aghast. "We don't know *that*. He might have done a bunk as far as we know."

"Good point," Wish-Wash said. "The bowls club should never have elected him treasurer."

"What?" Oodles said. "You reckon he might have skipped town with all their money? You muppet! How much money do you think they raise from their afternoon teas?"

Wish-Wash raised his palms. "You're right. We shouldn't judge him too harshly." He looked up at Wendy. "He could walk in any minute, so you better make sure his share of biscuits are on the plate just to be safe."

At that moment, the curtains swished, which made them all turn.

But it clearly wasn't James — unless he had come in disguise as someone 50 years younger and wearing a summery dress.

"Katy!" Oodles said. "Everything all right?"

"I'm on the way home to check on Joffa. I've just swung by for a takeaway cuppa."

"Is that all you want, love?" Wendy asked.

Katy O'Fury nodded, and Wendy disappeared through the swinging doors into the kitchen.

"I'm just glad it wasn't Joffa who was injured." Then she realised what she had said. "Oh, that doesn't mean I don't feel for Moose."

"No offence taken," Oodles said. "It must have also been traumatic for Joffa. Hopefully, he'll feel better after a good night's sleep. Give Wish-Wash a bell at the museum if you need anything."

Katy looked at him oddly. "Funny you should say that. When I phoned the museum trying to find out what was going on, a stammering American answered the phone. Where does he fit in?"

Wish-Wash squeezed his eyes shut. "That would be Awesome Sauce."

"Is that supposed to mean something to me?" Katy said.

"His full name is Tim Noah the Fourth," Oodles said.

Katy poked her tongue into her cheek as she looked from face to face.

"I guess you'd be too young to remember his grandfather coming to town," Oodles said. "Tim Noah Junior? The billionaire who employed Moose and who wanted to buy the orchard where the museum is now?"

She shook her head.

"He's the one Gus Foot deals with in the United States. Bushranger Whiskers? The ones you cut for him?"

"So why is his grandson here? Has he still got designs on the land?"

Oodles shrugged. "If he has, he's not saying. But we have an open mind. His grandfather might still want to build a theme park on the site."

"Hey, that's what we can do!" Wish-Wash said.

"What?" Oodles said. "Pull down the museum and build our own theme park?"

Wish-Wash looked at him as if he were crazy. "Why would we do that when we are on the cusp of catching a flamin' Tasmanian Tiger and becoming famous? I meant we can visit Disneyland Paris?"

"I thought you said we were going to Donegal in Ireland?"

"It's in the same neighbourhood, isn't it!"

Katy was standing open-mouthed when Wendy came through with a tray carrying a yellow teapot, two mugs, a plate with six chocolate digestive biscuits and Katy's tea in a styrofoam cup.

"Careful a fly doesn't fly in, love," she said as she started transferring everything on to the table.

"I'm glad you're here as a witness," Katy said. "Because I think I'm starting to hear things."

Oodles shook his head. "No, you heard right. Wish-Wash and I are *probably* going to Ireland together. He won a trip for two by doing a DNA test."

Wendy gasped. "Why wasn't I told?"

"No one knew," Wish-Wash said. "I only told Oodles yesterday. Did you know I'm going as his carer."

"That's what *he* thinks." Oodles prodded his chest. "I'm the only one who has even been on a plane."

"Admit it, you're scared to go on a plane now," Wish-Wash said.

"I just have a healthy respect for the law of averages. It's different for you. No one ever gets in a plane crash their first time."

"All the more reason to take me as your carer. Look on me as your good-luck charm!"

Katy's eyes widened. "And when are you going on this trip?"

"In a bit less than four weeks," Wish-Wash said.

Katy looked from Wish-Wash to Oodles. "So you've already got your passports?"

"I have. Madge and I were planning another big trip before, you know . . . " Oodles spun his wedding ring on his finger.

She looked at Wish-Wash. "And you?"

"Do I even need a passport at my age? It's not like I'm a threat to anyone."

Katy folded her arms. "Every overseas traveller needs a passport, and you need to get on to it quickly. I think they take at least three weeks, so it's going to be touch and go."

Wish-Wash looked at Oodles. "You never told me that?"

"And what about SmartTraveller?" Katy said.

"Come again?" Oodles said.

"You must have heard of it? You register with the government. They send you travel advice, like where it's not safe to go, and they can locate your whereabouts in the event of disaster or emergency."

"What a waste of taxpayers' money!" Oodles said. "Madge always used to just tell her sister where we were going. Prue was the one who used to say, 'Oh, I wouldn't go there.'"

Katy picked up her takeaway cup. "I don't know why I volunteer for this stuff but I'll get straight on to researching travel requirements for you in the morning."

———

"Drink up quickly, old cock," Oodles said after Katy had left.

He was watching Wish-Wash pour tea into the mugs. Wendy was standing by with her cloth in case he spilled a bit.

"What's the hurry?" Wish-Wash said. "Do you want me to catch your indigestion, cobber?"

"We have to see a man about a dog."

"Again?"

Wendy went through the swinging doors to the kitchen, and Oodles watched her until she had vanished from sight.

He leaned across the table and whispered. "Don't take me so literally. It's Norm we have to go see. I just didn't want Big Ears to know about it."

"Big ears? Wendy hasn't got big ears. Big knockers, maybe? Why do we need to see Norm?"

"Can't you keep your voice down? Gawdsake! Norm might have an update on James."

Wish-Wash lowered his voice. "And you don't want Wendy to know about that?" He dunked one of the biscuits in his tea three times as if he were giving the matter deep thought, then he looked up. "Why not?"

"Have you ever thought Wendy might know more about James's disappearance than she's letting on?"

"No." Wish-Wash loudly sucked the tea out of his biscuit, then used a hand to wipe soggy crumbs from his lips. "Why would I?"

"You never heard of kidnapping? James's wealthy family would likely pay a bob or two for him."

Wish-Wash looked at the kitchen door that had stopped swinging. "You really think Wendy had something to do with his disappearance?"

"Do I have to remind you she has criminal connections? Hubby in jail, a dwindling customer base . . . "

"You really think Gordo has turned into a criminal mastermind working from his prison HQ? Our Gordo? The bloke who couldn't even cook a steak without burning it."

Oodles sat back, and exhaled noisily. "You're probably right. But loose lips do sink ships."

"First dogs, now ships. Why are you speaking in code today?"

"I just don't think we should tell the whole world we're off to ask Norm about James."

"Wendy is hardly the whole world!"

"Strewth! You know how this cafe works? It's like Chinese Whispers Central Station. Wendy blabs to half a dozen customers every hour, they each go out and blab to six others. Before you know it, the whole state knows we're going to see Norm."

Wish-Wash looked at his watch. "I really have to get back to the museum."

Oodles rapped his index finger on the table, like punctuation marks. "This" *(tap)* "is" *(tap)* "important".

"More important than running our business?"

"Awesome Sauce is holding the fort, isn't he?"

"Holding the fort isn't the problem. Every time I leave the room he changes the fort around."

"Look, at his age he's bound to know a lot more than you about the computer. Why don't you take advantage of that rather than fighting it?"

Wish-Wash dunked another biscuit and stared at it as he held it above his cup. The drips made *plop, plop, plop* noises and Oodles figured Wish-Wash would open his trap when he was finished thinking.

When he did, the words came rushing out. "It's escalated beyond the computer though, hasn't it!"

"How?"

"Why do you think I made him disengage the doorbell?"

"I really have no idea. In case you haven't noticed I've got more urgent things on my mind than *ding* blinking *dong*."

"That's the point. It doesn't go *ding dong* when people come in now."

Oodles frowned. "What noise does it make?"

"It roars."

"It roars?"

"Like a Tiger."

Oodles slapped a palm on the table. "Why didn't we think of that?"

"What's with the sitting-down happy dance?" Wish-Wash said. "You haven't heard me out?"

"Go on then, I'm listening."

"Awesome Sauce got in early this morning, and I thought he could mind the desk while I finished the crossword. Who knew, though, two down, seven letters, starts with P would take me so long to work out? When I came back downstairs, the kid was smiling but I didn't know why until V arrived for work. Blow me down, the door roared like a Tiger when she came in."

"I'm still not getting this? Maybe we should start paying the American to reward him for his ingenuity?"

"Over my dead body! You know where he got the soundbite of the Tiger? He downloaded it from the internet. But the thing is, it's not from a Tasmanian Tiger. It's from a Bengal Tiger!"

———

Wish-Wash paused at the kerb and looked for coming cars.

"Where d'ya think you're going?" Oodles said.

"It was your idea to go see Norm."

Oodles shook his head. "You won't find *The Pick of the Crop* offices across the road any more."

"Since when?"

"Since at least 10 years ago when they moved!"

Wish-Wash scratched his whiskers. "Did they outgrow their premises?"

"The reverse. Why would they bother paying rent for a skeleton staff to rattle around in that big space?"

Norm had come the full circle, but the circle was much smaller than it used to be.

He had started his working life as a cadet journalist on *The Pick of the Crop* in the 1990s when it was a thriving daily print newspaper with two dozen staff.

When the newspaper was downgraded to a weekly print publication, it required fewer journalists but Norm was one of the lucky middle-ranked reporters who kept their jobs.

He wasn't in such a good position when it went solely online. By then Norm was a senior hand who was paid a much-higher salary.

He didn't mind getting the tap on the shoulder.

He got a good redundancy payout that he invested in buying the newsagency across the road from the museum.

The irony was the newsagency didn't have many actual newspapers to sell any more, so he had turned it into an e-agency. But the bottom had fallen out of that market too, and *The Pick of the Crop* had taken him back on a much-reduced wage as editor, and the sole full-time employee.

"So, where are their offices these days?" Wish-Wash asked.

Oodles pointed to his right. "About half a mile past the town limits. Next to the sewerage treatment works and opposite the tip."

Wish-Wash screwed up his face.

The tip wasn't bad in these days of recycling and rapid landfill. But the sewerage treatment plant was as pongy as it was when it opened for business 30-odd years ago.

Guess who the mayor was then?

James had pushed the costly project with all his political weight.

He argued that unless taxpayers accepted the hefty levy, Windy Mountain folk faced even heftier bills up the track to repair their crumbling and outmoded sewerage system.

The location of the sewerage treatment works had been even more controversial than its price-tag.

The logical thing would have been to site it nearer to the centre of town to cut down on the pipes that needed to be laid. But logic didn't enter into it. That part of town was where the Northan mansion was.

Even more perplexing was the name it came to be known by. If local naming convention had been followed, it would have been dubbed the Colonel Richard Northan Memorial Sewerage Works in line with every other major landmark in the town.

Instead, Oodles, then still working for the council, was ordered to put a sign up declaring it was the Slutz Plains Sewerage Treatment Plant even though it had nothing to do with the next town.

"I really haven't got time for this," Wish-Wash said as he trudged behind Oodles.

"Relax," Oodles said. "What more damage can Awesome Sauce do?"

Wish-Wash shook his head. "I hate to think."

As he said this, they both saw a wild-haired man with a German shepherd walking towards them.

Everyone just called the man Messerschmitt.

He had turned up at the pub a bit over two years ago with that no-good Freddy Cuthbert. Now he was a part of the bar furniture.

Oodles stopped and turned towards the kerb.

"I thought you said there was no point crossing?" Wish-Wash said.

"You can see as well as I can who's coming."

"That dog looks ferocious but I've never heard that he bites."

"His owner probably could do some damage with those rotten teeth of his."

Wish-Wash puffed out his chest. "Messerschmitt doesn't scare me, especially when there are two of us."

Oodles turned his head briefly as he crossed the road. "Please yourself. But there is only one now."

He could hear the quickening footsteps behind him, and he wasn't surprised when he reached the other side and turned to see the green shirt in close pursuit and the unshaven Messerschmitt walking past them on the other side. "Don't turn around," Oodles hissed. "He'll just think we're looking at him."

"Isn't that what you're doing?"

"But I'm trying not to make it look obvious."

They began walking towards the sewerage treatment plant again.

"You know he as good as stole that dog, don't you?" Wish-Wash said. "Jacko wasn't keen on him having a pup, but what could he say when Messerschmitt stared him down."

"Yes, that's what I heard too."

"So who do you think kidnapped Jimbo?"

Oodles threw his arm out to stop Wish-Wash, and eyeballed him as they stood on the footpath. "I never said he's been kidnapped for sure. I just think we should keep an open mind, and not broadcast our moves to Wendy. I'm hoping our face-to-face meeting with Norm will make him take us more seriously because I don't think he sounded all that perturbed over the phone. We need him to track down that spare key."

They walked to the town's outskirts, which is where the footpath ran out.

They continued single-file on the verge of the road, dodging potholes, and trying not to get caught up in the blackberries that skirted the road.

A log truck went past them with a whoosh of air that tested the ability of Oodles's hair cream to hold everything in place. He stopped and turned. "I think we better cross the road."

Wish-Wash snarled: "We just crossed to this side!"

"It's safer to face oncoming traffic. Weren't you ever a Boy Scout?"

Wish-Wash scratched his head. "I was, actually. But I don't remember being taught road sense. I only recollect the useless stuff they taught. Do you know how many times I've had to tie a square knot? Or climb a tree at my age?"

"I remember being told to always walk on the right side of the road. Stay here if you want, I'm crossing."

Seeing the way was clear, that's what he did. The dib-dib-dib, dob-dob-dob noises told him Wish-Wash was right behind him.

When he walked a bit further he saw two metal stumps sticking out of the ground on the verge beside the road. He stopped and shook his head.

"What are you looking at?" Wish-Wash said.

"You must know this is where the sign used to welcome people to Windy Mountain." Oodles shook his head again. "It looks like someone took a hacksaw to it. Bloody vandals."

Wish-Wash pinched his nose. "Anyone would think someone had stolen your life-savings the way you look. It's only a flamin' sign." He started walking again. "When they replace the sign, they should call this place Stink City."

When they reached the edge of the sewerage treatment plant a bit further along, the footpath suddenly started again.

The footpath was the result of more stupid decisions of the learned men of council. Who would ever come out here to promenade?

The ponds were visible through the mesh-wire fence.

Wish-Wash stopped, pinched his nose again, and pointed to the *no trespassing* sign. "Why do they even need that? Why do they even need a fence? No self-respecting burglar is going to run the pong gauntlet. The council's got more money than good sense. If they had bothered to ask me I would have just told them to hang up another sign. *No turds kept on these premises.*"

"You do go on," Oodles pushed him forward. "Norm's office is just on the other side."

A double-storey building clad in galvanised iron came into sight.

Norm was tapping on a computer on the other side of the vast room when the old men walked in.

Last time Oodles had been to the old offices of *The Pick of the Crop*, he had to get past a receptionist, a frosted-glass security door and then a secretary to see Dobber Leggs. But apparently the new company didn't think the incoming editor needed any protection, apart from the deterrent of stinkiness.

Norm looked up, and stopped typing on his computer as they walked towards him. "Gents! What brings you here?"

"We're still worried about James," Oodles said. "Heard from him yet?"

Norm shook his head. "Didn't I say I'd let you know if I did!"

"We now think he's been kidnapped," Wish-Wash said.

Norm stood up like someone bouncing up from a seat booby-trapped with tacks.

Oodles turned on Wish-Wash. "Did you have to go and say that?"

"You said it yourself. It might be true."

Norm rolled his eyes. "As if I didn't have enough to worry about!" He put a hand under his chin. "I'm already up to here with it."

"That figures," Wish-Wash said. "It's hardly surprising when your office is next to the shit farm. You know it really stinks in here?"

"You think I don't know that?" Norm's voice dripped with sarcasm. "The location is one of the perks of the job. It's right up there with no staff. It's not about *making* money these days, it's about *saving* money."

He pointed to assorted bits of paper on his desk.

"Bad enough I have to wade through all the place-getters in the show society produce market. Now someone has stolen another sign, and you're adding kidnap to the list!"

"No, we're not." Oodles glared at Wish-Wash, then he realised what Norm had just said. "What sign?"

"The one outside the Colonel Richard Northan Memorial Rose Garden," Norm said.

Oodles looked around at Wish-Wash again.

"Why are you looking at me? Bad enough Jimbo accuses me of stealing flowers from that place, stealing the sign is definitely not my caper!"

"I wasn't accusing you of anything. I'm just thinking, can you believe it? First the town boundary signs, now this. What's going on?"

Wish-Wash shrugged. "Maybe someone is collecting them to cut out a ransom note?"

Oodles looked at him quizzically.

Wish-Wash pointed to the editor. "Tell him, Norm."

When nothing came from Norm, Wish-Wash said, "Haven't either of you seen those movies where the kidnappers snip letters out of the local newspaper and stick them together to say something like, '*Pay us $1 million in unmarked bills by midnight or James Northan gets it.*'"

Wish-Wash looked from blank face to blank face. "Do I have to spell everything out? Windy Mountain doesn't have a newspaper any more.

Not really. It's all on-line. Hence the disappearing signs. The kidnappers are obviously collecting words for their wooden ransom note."

"That's got to be the silliest thing I've ever heard," Oodles said.

Wish-Wash stroked his whiskers. "Yeah, you're probably right. If kidnappers had had to put up with Jimbo this long, they'd be the ones wanting to give us $1 million if we'd take him back."

Oodles tutt-tutted. "That's a terribly insensitive thing to say in front of his son-in-law."

Norm held out his outstretched hands. "It's OK, really. I know exactly where you're coming from, Wish-Wash. Don't tell Maddie, but for the life of me, I don't know how he ever got anyone to vote for him."

"Let's not get carried away," Oodles said. "He might just have gone off somewhere to try to write the perfect poem."

"Maybe," Norm said. "But to be honest, he still has a big learning curve to travel. James is still at the *roses are red, violets are blue* stage. Wherever he is, he's more likely to come up with the perfect limerick than the perfect sonnet."

Oodles swung around and eyeballed Wish-Wash. "Look, I know I was the one who raised the possibility of kidnap, but we really have no evidence."

"That might leave suicide though."

Wish-Wash was caught in a crossfire of glares. "What did I say now? You saw it yourself, Oodles. That note in the kitchen might well be a suicide note."

"Wish-Wash!" Oodles scowled. "What did I say about insensitivity?"

"It's OK," Norm said. "You grow a thick skin in this business. I can see you blokes are worried though, coming all this way. I'll have another look around for that key, so I can put everyone's mind at rest."

He resumed his seat. "In the meantime . . . I really am busy."

"So you haven't heard then?" Wish-Wash said.

Norm sighed heavily. "What now?"

"Moose is in hospital."

"What happened?"

"Him and Joffa were tracking an animal, and he tripped over a fallen tree and broke his leg."

Oodles tut-tutted again. "Strewth! We don't know that! It might just be a badly strained ankle."

"Go and see him for yourself," Wish-Wash said. "He's in the local hospital, upstairs."

"I-I-I don't know where I'll find the time."

"I forgot. You two have history!" Wish-Wash said.

"That was years ago," Oodles said. "I'm sure the big fella would have forgiven you by now."

"I dunno. He was pretty angry at the time." Norm looked down at the bare floorboards. "But that's really besides the point. I really am busy with this stolen sign and all."

Oodles folded his arms. "What does Stretch say?"

Norm sighed. "Sergeant Stretch is also bewildered. He's trying to work out what the signs have in common."

Wish-Wash looked at him blankly. "I think he might be over-thinking it. What they have in common is probably they're all signs."

Norm held his gaze. "Let's leave the police work to the police, shall we?"

But Wish-Wash wasn't finished yet. "Here's some more news you might want to report, Norm. I'm taking Oodles to Ireland soon."

———

The sign outside the sewerage treatment plant caught Oodles's attention straight away.

He grabbed Wish-Wash by the shoulder to bring him to a halt. "Did you notice that before we went in?"

Wish-Wash didn't reply. His face was turning blue because he probably didn't want to open his mouth to breathe.

It wasn't so much a new sign, but an old one which had been tied to the fence with wire where the *Slutz Plains Sewerage Treatment Plant* sign used to be. The wording had been doctored to say: *The Colonel Richard Northan Memorial ON-THE-N* ose *Garden.*

"You reckon someone erected it while we were in seeing Norm?" Oodles said.

"Hard to say," Wish-Wash exhaled as he spoke and his nose wrinkled as he sucked in some air. "I can tell you this for nothing though. The Slutz Plains Council is going to be mightily annoyed when they learn they don't own the sewerage plant any more."

"They never actually owned it, you muppet. James was just trying to needle them."

"You sure?" Wish-Wash steepled his hands to cover his mouth and nose. "If I die of a lethal disease, it'll give you something to think about on the long plane ride to Ireland on your own."

Oodles shrugged. "I thought you were intent on out-living James?"

Wish-Wash surrendered one of his hands to point to one of the ponds. "With any luck, he's drowned himself. It's the way Shakespeare would have ended it. A comedy dressed up as a tragedy. *Jimbo, wherefore art thou?"*

Oodles chewed a fingernail. "Let's not get sidetracked. Was this sign here before, or not?"

Wish-Wash shrugged. "I don't know about you but I wasn't admiring the scenery last time we passed." He waved a hand in front of his face. "Boy, it sure does stink here. Makes you feel sorry for Jimbo." He glanced over to the ponds. "What a way to go, eh?"

"Will you cut it out. I need to know what you think about the sign." Oodles glanced up at the fence and took a long look before exhaling noisily. "It's a lot of words not to notice." He pointed. "Look at the way they've scrunched up the words *ON-THE-N?* Surely that would have caught one of our eyes?"

"My eyes were focused on the finish-li . . . " Wish-Wash stopped mid-sentence and Oodles could nearly hear the cogs in his brain turning.

"Who loves ya, baby!" Wish-Wash said in his best Kojak impersonation. "I should have seen it straight away. Scrub my suicide theory. I've just worked out who the kidnapper is."

"Not again! I wish I had never put the kidnap thought in your head! What don't you understand about holding off speculating on anything until we have actual evidence?"

"Can't you see? This *is* evidence. It just strengthens my theory the kidnappers are collecting signs so they can compile a ransom note."

Oodles peered up at the sign. "How do you figure that? If this is any indication, they're just changing the location of the signs. This might have nothing to do with James's disappearance. We might just be dealing with a practical joker. We'll know for sure if the town boundary signs turn up at opposite ends of the town. Population 3003 becomes 3004, and vice-versa."

Wish-Wash shook his head slowly. "See, this is why you're such a lousy Scrabble player."

"What's that got to do with the price of eggs?"

"Sometimes in Scrabble you strategically trade in some of your letters because you know the Z you need hasn't been claimed yet."

"And how would you know that if you're not cheating by sneaking looks at what other people have got?"

"Can't you see? The kidnappers didn't have to cheat. They already knew the sewerage works sign had the Z they needed." He smiled. "Slutz Plains."

"You're drawing a long bow, if you ask me."

"But am I? It's my deduction we even saw the kidnapper in the vicinity."

"Who?"

"Messerschmitt."

"Come off the grass! Messerschmitt was nowhere near here."

"He was coming from this direction. And you have to admit, he did have a guilty look about him."

"He always looks like that. You're the one who thought Messerschmitt was perfectly harmless when we passed him. Now you're accusing him of kidnapping James!"

"I didn't say he was harmless. All I said is I'm not scared of him. But I am allowed to change my mind, aren't I? I'm only doing what police on TV do all the time. As new evidence comes to hand, they reconsider the facts."

Oodles turned. "C'mon, let's go. I'm starting to think the pong here is having a detrimental effect on your thinking."

Wish-Wash caught him up in two strides. "Have you got a better idea?"

"Yeah. I'll walk you back to the museum, see what Awesome Sauce is up to."

Wish-Wash ran his fingers through his hair. "You had to go and remind me why I didn't want to leave him alone for so long."

————

When the old men arrived back at the museum, they braced themselves before going inside.

To their surprise, the doorbell was still silent.

It was only when he turned around, Oodles got a fright. Sitting on the bench across the street was a familiar face.

Oodles pointed a trembling finger. "What's *he* doing sitting there?"

Wish-Wash turned. "Oh, he's just waiting for the pub next door to us to open."

"But it's *our* bench. You, me and James are the only ones who ever sit on it."

Wish-Wash shrugged. "Messerschmitt often sits on the bench in the afternoon."

"Doesn't it worry you? You're the one who thinks he's a kidnapper who is stealing all the signs. Aren't you worried he'll steal our bench too?"

"That old thing? He's welcome to it! You're the only one who thinks it's still some kind of sacred monument. It's become an eyesore. The council hasn't given it a lick of paint in years and some vandal . . .

" He turned to the Texan kid. "I won't say who . . . has taken a pocketknife to it."

Oodles stiffened. "You know fine well I had good reason for doing that." He addressed Awesome Sauce. "That bench used to be one of the council's prized possessions."

"Maybe," Wish-Wash said. "But they haven't given a toss about it since they relocated it to this end of the town."

"It still bears the name of Colonel Northan."

"Do you think they really care? Now the shiny Colonel Richard Northan Memorial has pride of place? Messerschmitt would be doing the town a favour." Wish-Wash let that statement hang in the air, then added, "But trust me, he's just waiting for The Applecart to open."

FIVE
HELP ME TAKE IT THROUGH THE NIGHT
WEDNESDAY MORNING

OODLES TOSSED and turned all night.

Wish-Wash just didn't understand how he felt about that bench.

He had never tried to hide he was the one vandalising it. But to be fair, he was only recording the number of times he was fulfilling Madge's dying wish.

His childhood sweetheart had been driving her friends home from a bowls tournament when a bushfire jumped the highway. Despite her terrible burns, she lived long enough to make him swear to go to mass each Sunday.

He kept the pledge — reluctantly.

But he carved a new notch on the bench in broad daylight every Monday to mark his attendances, like a prisoner marking off time on the wall of his cell.

He had stopped doing it now.

But to him the pock-marked bench was a sacred shrine. Why couldn't Wish-Wash understand that?

Adding fuel to his fitful night were thoughts about what terrible thing might have befallen James. The Mayor had never given him cause to actually like him, but that was irrelevant. Wish-Wash didn't get that either. Old folk really had to look out for each other.

Oodles woke up exhausted at 6.30am.

He washed the sleep out of his eyes with a flannel, cleaned his dentures and dressed. He made himself a pot of tea, and ate his cereal beneath the clock on the living room wall. That clock had been a retirement present for Madge from the hospital auxiliary. It didn't seem fair she was gone, the clock wasn't, and he wasn't.

After breakfast, he sat on a chair near the back door and put on his shoes, which was a task that got harder every day. He went into the backyard where Gough was bouncing up and down at the end of his chain.

"Ready for walkies, boy?"

As usual, they walked down to the High Street.

Wendy must have forgotten to bring in the sign on the footpath, because The Wind Tunnel Cafe was never open at this time of the morning. Unless she was now touting for early-morning trade? She had extended her hours lately in the hunt for more customers. He looked in the window, but saw only two empty tables in the half light.

Gough pulled him towards the kerb. The dog couldn't wait to get over to the base of the Colonel Northan statue for a sniff and a pee.

No matter how often he did it, it always made Oodles's day.

Oodles smiled as Gough cocked his leg.

Gough wagged his tail as he towed Oodles the rest of the way across the road to the park.

After Gough did his excavations, they headed back through the gate to the High Street and walked towards the Tasmanian Tiger Museum.

He tied Gough to a post on the footpath, and went in.

As he crossed the threshold, a deep voice told him he was now entering the Twilight Zone.

Tim Noah and Wish-Wash looked up from behind the reception desk. Both of them were chuckling, but Wish-Wash was also pointing.

Oodles assumed at first he was gesturing towards the door chime above the door, which was now playing eerie music.

But then he realised he was pointing to something outside.

———

Oodles turned, half-expecting to see Gough off his leash and bounding across the road.

But what he saw was the Colonel Northan Memorial Bench was gone!

"Aren't we lucky?" Wish-Wash said behind him. "Some bugger *has* removed the eyesore."

Oodles turned to face him as the heat rose to his face. "I told you Messerschmitt was up to no good."

"We have no evidence it was him."

"It never occurred to you he was casing the joint? Nothing to do with waiting for the pub to open? He was working out when and how to strike?"

"You're the one who says we shouldn't jump to conclusions. Don't you want to consider other possibilities?"

"Listen to yourself!" Oodles turned again and gazed at the void. When he heard a noise he spun around and saw one of the Korean twins filling the urn.

"Get this old bloke a cup of tea and a chair, V, before he has a heart attack." Wish-Wash said. "I don't fancy flying all the way to Ireland with a corpse."

"You just worry about yourself." Oodles ran his hand over his clammy forehead as he walked over to a table laid out for customers with a red-checkered tablecloth and a small wicker basket full of sugar satchels.

"Look, I'm the one who should be the most upset. I know we've both sat on that bench many times, but I'm the only one who has slept on it."

Oodles sat down. Fair dinkum, what did Wish-Wash look like today? An elderly ball boy at Wimbledon in his purple and green shirt.

"Ask Awesome Sauce," Wish-Wash said. "I was as surprised as you when I saw it had gone." Wish-Wash pinched the bridge of his nose. "Not that he was a great help. That voice you heard when you came in was his idea of a joke."

Awesome Sauce held his palms up in the act of surrender. "I was just trying to lighten thangs up."

"You bloody dingbat," Wish-Wash said. "I never actually said an alien spaceship had sucked up the bench in search for intelligent life. All I said was it would be a good plot line for a Sci-Fi novel."

"You *are* joking!" Oodles rolled his eyes. "The only alien you need to consider is called Messerschmitt."

"Dunno," Wish-Wash said. "The more I think about it he *must* have kidnapped Jimbo. But the bench?" He shook his head. "That doesn't make sense."

Oodles drained his tea until he saw nothing but tea-leaves. "You're so sure Messerschmitt has kidnapped James and stolen the signs, yet you don't like him for stealing our bench. How come, Gawdsake?"

"Simple. It's got no writing on it."

"It's got a bronze plaque with embossed writing."

"What are they going to do? Cut out one of those letters with a blowtorch and risk burning off a finger? No, I reckon what we have here is a coincidence. Obviously, we have two different perpetrators."

Oodles shook his head.

"Hear me out. I've been thinking this through," Wish-Wash said. "I think Slutz Plains must have stolen our bench as some kind of revenge because they are annoyed they lost ownership of the sewerage works."

Oodles squeezed his eyes shut. When he opened them, Wish-Wash was smiling.

"You can't be serious?" Oodles said.

"They probably couldn't have done it on their own either. I reckon Windy Mountain Council helped them."

"Now you really are away with the fairies!"

"You got any better ideas?"

"Yes, Messerschmitt. I told you."

"He has no motive."

"Criminals like Messerschmitt don't need motives. They pull the wings off flies just for the fun of it."

Wish-Wash sat down behind the reception desk and slapped a hand loudly on the bench. "The council has been waiting for that old bench to fall apart for years. They haven't even tried to maintain it since the statue of Colonel Northan was built on the main drag. I think they're ashamed of the bench now, that's why they relocated it to this end of town."

Oodles examined Wish-Wash's face. "You really think the council must have taken it away?"

"It's possible."

"In the middle of the night?" Oodles's eyes widened. "Those tight buggers never paid *me* overnight penalty rates."

Wish-Wash chewed on an imaginary lollipop. "Who loves ya, baby?"

"Enough of the Kojak-isms. If Messerschmitt thinks he can get away with theft, he has another thing coming. I'm going to see Sergeant Stretch." He banged his fist on the table, and his empty cup would have bounced over the edge of the table if V hadn't caught it.

———

"How did it go with Stretch?" Wish-Wash asked when they waited for their tea in the cafe a few hours later.

Oodles screwed up his face. "He wasn't even there. The police station was closed."

"You don't think whoever nicked the bench has also nicked the policemen?"

"You muppet! Someone had taped a sign to the door saying they'd be *Back in 30 Minutes.*"

"Did you wait?"

"Yes. I waited for 45 minutes but then I had to come here."

"That's a stroke of luck, then. It saved you from embarrassing yourself."

"Messerschmitt can't get away with stealing our bench!"

"You have no proof! Coppers go by the rule book. Stretch would think you're a crazy old codger."

"You can talk! Do you have evidence Messerschmitt kidnapped James?"

"He stole the signs, didn't he?"

"We don't know that."

"Mark my words, we'll get a ransom note from him sooner or later incorporating bits of those signs." Wish-Wash frowned. "I'm not sure Messerschmitt has thought it through though."

"Why not?"

"I can't see anyone shelling out much to save the Mayor, can you?"

"What are you talking about? His daughter would. Everyone knows the Northan family is loaded."

Wish-Wash shook his head again. "If the family is so well off, why is Norm working next to the shit farm? Why isn't he lying in a hammock strung between oak trees in that enormous backyard of theirs?"

Oodles picked up the sugar bowl and twirled it absent-mindedly. "I just wish you'd make up your mind! I can't keep track. One minute you suspect suicide, the next kidnap, then you have doubts about even that."

Wish-Wash scowled at him. "You're the one who thought of kidnap first." He stabbed a finger towards the sugar bowl in Oodles's fidgety hands. "One thing I think we can both agree on is you don't even use sugar. So I want that back when my tea arrives."

Two women were suddenly bearing down on them from different directions.

One came through the front door, clutching a satchel. The other came from the kitchen, carrying a tray.

Wendy reached the old men's table first and Wish-Wash looked up at her. "Better get another cup for Katy."

Katy put the bulging satchel on the table and smiled at Wendy. "It's OK, I'm only staying for a minute."

"You don't have to explain to me, love," Wendy said. "If I was married to Joffa, I'd want to get home and make up for lost time too."

"If you must know, Joffa's catching up on lost sleep. It's the salon I have to get back to." Katy looked down to the old men. "I've just popped in to deliver your passport-application papers."

Alarm came over Wish-Wash's face as he looked at the thick satchel. "How many flamin' forms are there?"

"Not as many as you think. Most of what's here are pamphlets I found about Ireland."

Wendy shook her head. "I still can't believe you blokes are going that far. What will I tell James when he finally turns up? Can you imagine his face when I tell him you've buggered off to Ireland?"

"We think he's been kidnapped," Wish-Wash said.

Oodles looked at the ceiling. "Wish-Wash is all on his own with that theory."

Wish-Wash glared at him. "You haven't come up with a better explanation."

"I have lots of possible reasons." Oodles started counting them out on his fingers. "1. He's with Maddie. 2. He's gone on a writer's retreat. 3. He's visiting a rich auntie before she dies . . . shall I go on?"

Wish-Wash looked puzzled. "You never told me about his rich auntie? Crikey, she must be a fair age!"

"She's only hypothetical, you muppet. My point is there might be a hundred reasons the Mayor is not here. That's what I was going to tell you when I dropped into the museum this morning, only we got sidetracked with the bench."

"What about the bench?" Katy said.

"Someone has nicked it," Wish-Wash said, smiling.

"Lucky Gordo's got an alibi," Wendy said.

"We think Messerschmitt did it," Oodles said.

"Speak for yourself." Wish-Wash's voice rose. "I think he only took the signs."

"What signs?" Katy said.

"You haven't heard?" Oodles said. "Someone's nicked the town-limit signs and the sign outside the rose garden? I imagine all the details are in *The Pick of the Crop*."

"Who reads the paper now it's only online?" Katy said.

Wendy swept a hand across her brow. "I repeat. I can safely say Gordo couldn't have done any of it."

Wish-Wash looked up at her. "You do know he's matey with Freddy Cuthbert who happens to be a mate of Messerschmitt's?"

"What? And you reckon Gordo put Messerschmitt up to it?" Wendy rolled her eyes. "That ratbag has never even visited my hubby in jail, so how are they even in touch? Mental telepathy?"

Oodles rubbed a hand over the back of his neck. "No one is accusing Gordo, Wendy."

Wish-Wash glared at him. "You're the one who says we should have an open mind."

"Not that blinking open!" Oodles said. "Let's just assume Messer-schmitt was acting on his own when he stole the bench."

"Here we go again! You're so sure about *your* evidence but you're not willing to consider Jimbo might have been kidnapped or has topped himself."

Oodles looked apologetically from Katy to Wendy. "Suicide is another of Wish-Wash's wild theories. I just can't see it, can you? James has got too much to be proud about in this town."

"He's *never* been proud of *us*," Wish-Wash said.

"But why would he end it all by drowning himself in one of the sewerage treatment ponds?"

Oodles saw the shock on Katy's face. "I should have explained," he said. "That was Wish-Wash's theory *yesterday*. Ask me about his new theory *tomorrow*. We know who he thinks stole the signs. But can you guess who he thinks nicked the bench?"

Katy shook her head.

"The Slutz Plains Council, that's who."

"It's possible," Wish-Wash said. "I reckon they're working in cahoots with the Windy Mountain Council."

Oodles tut-tutted.

Wish-Wash looked up at Katy. "If you didn't know the signs were even missing, you couldn't know one has turned up doctored at the sewerage works. It implies the plant now belongs to Windy Mountain, not Slutz Plains any more."

Oodles closed his eyes and shook his head slowly.

Wish-Wash poured the tea. "You're just jealous that I'm a realist, cobber. Have you even checked with the Windy Mountain Council to see if they removed the bench?"

"Have you?"

"You're the one with the council contacts. You should be able to find out if they've done a clandestine deal with Slutz Plains."

Oodles scoffed. "They'd only think I had lost all my marbles if I suggested that."

Katy turned to go. "You'll need to fill in the passport application, Wish-Wash, as soon as you can. You'll also need two passport photos."

Wish-Wash's eyes popped. "Where the heck will I get those done around here?"

Katy pointed out one end of the window. "The Slutz Plains travel agency also does passport photos. I was up there this morning getting the forms and the pamphlets."

Wish-Wash reached over and reclaimed the sugar bowl. "Since when have they had a travel agency?"

Oodles watched him shovel four teaspoons into his tea. "For blinking years."

Wish-Wash looked up. "Why are you speaking to me like I'm a moron? I only ever go to Slutz Plains to see what nice clothes the opportunity shop has in."

"So you had your dalliance with Billy's mother in a fitting room, did you?"

"Don't even joke about that!"

"I'd give you a lift over there, only I really have to get back to the salon," Katy said.

"A likely story," Wendy said. "Wink-wink nudge-nudge, say no more."

Katy rolled her eyes. "Perhaps you want to come give me a hand CUTTING HAIR. I had to shut the salon early yesterday because of everything. Joffa went straight to bed ON HIS OWN when he returned from the hospital, but it was a good thing I was home because Norm Hit came knocking and wanted to interview him for the paper, and I had to wake him up again."

She disappeared through the bead curtains with a swish.

———

Oodles struggled to keep up with Wish-Wash as he bounded back towards the museum.

"Why did you think Norm went to see Joffa?" Wish-Wash asked.

"It was probably his way of getting the story of Moose's accident without having to speak to Moose." Oodles was losing ground. "Can't you slow down, old cock?"

Wish-Wash kept walking quickly but half-turned his head. "I thought you said Moose would have forgiven him by now?"

"I don't think Norm is brave enough to find out one way or another. Wait up, what's the hurry?"

Wish-Wash pulled up and waited for Oodles to draw level. "You'll have to walk faster than this when we go to Ireland."

"I won't have to. You're sure to walk more slowly when you're carrying two heavy suitcases."

Wish-Wash frowned. "I was only going to take one case."

"You're forgetting one of the duties of a carer is to carry the other person's case."

"Is it?" Wish-Wash screwed up his face like he was suffering from a sudden gastric pain. "I, er, don't have to go as your carer if you don't want me to."

"I thought you said Doc Jenkins was insisting on it?"

Wish-Wash pinched a fold of his camouflaged double chin, and gave this some thought for a moment. "You know doctors? I'd get a second opinion if I were you."

"I've been going to Doc Jenkins for years and he's always done right by me." Oodles said. "Are you having second thoughts?"

"About going to Ireland?"

"No, about going as my carer."

"Matter of fact I am. I don't care what that quack says. A man as fit and healthy and with-it as you ought to be able to carry his own suitcase."

With that, he turned and started walking at a fast gallop again.

"What's the hurry?" Oodles said.

"I need to read what Norm wrote about Moose in *The Pick of the Crop.*"

———

Wish-Wash was scowling at something above the glass door when Oodles caught up to him just inside the foyer.

Oodles immediately knew why. The feeble growling noise the sensor triggered sounded like an animal with a sore throat.

"What on earth is that supposed to be?" Oodles said.

Wish-Wash pointed to the computer, which appeared to be unmanned. "Ask him?"

Slowly, Awesome Sauce's backward cap emerged from behind the computer, and then he stuck his hands up above his head as if he were surrendering again. "You weren't supposed to hear that. I thought you'd be gone longer."

"Strewth," Oodles said. "What if someone else had come in and heard it? Whatever beast that is, it needs throat lozenges!"

"It's actually a snow leopard. I've been doing some research," Awesome Sauce said. "Listen."

Oodles heard a rattle of keys, then a robotic voice reciting from an internet page.

"The last-known Tasmanian Tiger, or Thylacine, as it is known scientifically, died at the Hobart zoo on September 7, 1936. Related to a kangaroo, it had a head like a wolf, and a backward-facing pouch like a wombat's."

Oodles stroked his chin. "Very impressive. Wish-Wash never said the computer could talk."

"The text-to-speech function isn't all that obvious. You don't know what you d0n't know, RIGHT?"

"I also don't know where it said the Tasmanian Tiger sounded anything like a snow leopard?"

Awesome Sauce shook his head. "The more I read, the more confused I got. The noise it made was variously described as a deep-throated bark, a grunt, a hiss, a blood-curdling squeal similar to the loud neighing of a horse, a yelp like that of a puppy, a grunt, a prolonged and very loud undulating bark, and a coughing bark."

"Don't ask me. I've never seen or heard one." Oodles looked at Wish-Wash. "What did the one in the bus shelter sound like?"

"Now you're testing me. It was so long ago. But if I was pushed, I'd have to go with the blood-curdling sound." Wish-Wash shook his fist towards the box above the door and shouted. "Nothing like that though. We'd be a laughing stock if anyone else heard that."

"I was experimenting, OK?" the young Texan said.

"Is that what you call it?" Wish-Wash said. "Maybe we should change our name to the Windy Mountain Snow Leopard Museum — as a flamin' *experiment*."

Oodles took Wish-Wash by the shoulder. "Calm down. Last thing we need is for you to blow a gasket." He looked back towards the desk. "I'm sure Awesome Sauce was trying his best."

"If that's the best he can do . . . "

Oodles squeezed Wish-Wash's shoulder harder. "If you get sick on me now, I might have to carry *your* suitcase."

That made Wish-Wash smile briefly, as if he was picturing it, but then his expression changed and he fixed his angry eyes back on

Awesome Sauce. He waved a finger. "I just hope you're able to turn that thing off."

"Easy as. Now?"

"If not, sooner." Wish-Wash walked towards the reception desk gate. "We need to use that computer."

"Perhaps Awesome Sauce can help us?" Oodles said.

Wish-Wash made a huffing noise as he went to the other side of the desk. "Frankly, I'm a bit sick of his help. I'm quite capable of finding the newspaper site myself."

"You sure?" the American said.

"Of course I'm sure." Wish-Wash looked over Awesome Sauce's shoulder as he speedily tapped the keys to disconnect the snow leopard from the chimes. "I've been reading *The Pick of the Crop* before you were a twinkle in your father's eye."

"But he hasn't seen it since it went on-line," Oodles added.

"Really?" Awesome Sauce looked up. "Is it free access or is it behind a paywall?"

The old men looked at each other.

"It used to cost 20 cents," Wish-Wash said blankly.

Awesome Sauce turned around and studied his face. "Are you sure you don't want me to help you?"

Wish-Wash looked back over to Oodles, then cleared his throat. "Well, since you're already sitting there . . . "

Awesome Sauce made another flurry of keystrokes as he got to work. Wish-Wash watched over his shoulder but Oodles knew there was no way he was keeping up. The only noise in the room for some minutes was the tap-tap-tapping on the keys.

"I have good news, and I have bad news," the Yankie kid finally said. "The site is protected by a firewall, which means you can only access it by paying a subscription. Good news is I can get round it if you want me to."

"Isn't hacking against the law?" Oodles said.

Wish-Wash looked over at him. "Have you turned over a new leaf."

"I've never committed a computer crime," Oodles hissed.

"Only because you don't own a computer," Wish-Wash said.

"Guys! Guys!" Awesome Sauce said. "I don't think this is going to trouble the FBI too much. We wouldn't be trying to break into NASA. All we'd be doing is having a sneak look at a local newspaper." He shrugged. "If they're silly enough to think a paywall affords them security . . . "

Wish-Wash raked his whiskers with the palm of his hand. "Do you think you can crack this?"

"Are you kidding? A schoolboy could get past this."

Wish-Wash rubbed the whiskers on the other side of his face. "Make it so, Mr Noah."

"Awesome Sauce, Captain, sir."

———

Oodles joined Wish-Wash on the other side of the counter. He was peering over Awesome Sauce's other shoulder when the article they were hunting flashed up on to the screen.

HUNTERS ON BRINK OF FINDING 'EXTINCT' TASMANIAN TIGER

One of the hunters at the Windy Mountain Tasmanian Tiger Museum is confident he will bring a live Thylacine out of the bush by week's end.

"We're going to prove once and for all this animal is not extinct," Jerome O'Fury told The Pick of the Crop.

Oodles couldn't believe his eyes. "I thought this story was supposed to be about Moose's accident?"

"So did I." Wish-Wash scanned the screen and they read on.

"We had a definite sighting of a Tasmanian Tiger we tracked to the other side of Bing Bong Mountain."

Wish-Wash buried his head in his hands. "Moose never said that. He only *suspected* it was a Tiger."

"We had to come back to Windy Mountain empty-handed because my partner tripped over a tree and hurt himself, but we plan to get back up there A.S.A.P. I have no doubt we'll soon have the prize we've wanted for so long."

No further mention of Moose was made in the lengthy article. That confirmed it for Oodles. Norm had been too scared to even go and see him.

Oodles threw his head into his hands. "Joffa, what have you done?"

———

Moose didn't look happy when they went to see him.

Not only was his leg now in a splint, by the look of his face he had already had words with Joffa, who was sitting by his bed with an even redder face.

Moose lifted his head from his pillow. "Why didn't that reporter come and see me, and get his story straight?"

Oodles sat down in the chair at the other side of the bed. "Didn't you threaten him with violence if he ever came near you again?"

"That was years ago," Moose said. "Besides . . . " He looked down at his leg. "It *is* busted, which means he'd be able to run away from me without too much trouble, anyway."

"Norm wasn't to know that. In all the years he had the e-agency across the road you never once set foot in there to make peace." Wish-Wash was still standing at the foot of the bed. Oodles pointed to the chair on the far side of the other bed, which was still unoccupied. "Why don't you grab that?"

"He seemed like such a decent fella, that reporter," Joffa said.

Oodles stared at him. "We didn't expect to even find you here. Aren't you supposed to be home asleep?"

Joffa ran a hand through his hair. "How can anyone sleep with the phone ringing all afternoon? I had no idea so many people read *The Pick of the Crop*."

Moose grimaced. It was hard to tell what was giving him the most pain. His leg or this fake news? "Why did you have to tell him we were certain it was a Tasmanian Tiger we were tracking?"

"I didn't. I tink I said you were *fairly* certain. I was still half asleep when he came round, so I can't recall precisely what I said. But I do remember that most of it was about you. How you tripped. How I helped you home. That's what I thought the whole article would be about."

"Thing is," Oodles said. "You'd think Norm would have plenty to fill his newspaper with without resorting to telling porkies. No one's heard hide nor hair from James."

"We now think he's been kidnapped by Messerschmitt," Wish-Wash said. He had dragged the chair over and positioned it near Moose's left knee.

"*We* do not." Oodles said. "Only *he* does."

"You know it makes sense." Wish-Wash looked from face to face. "Messerschmitt is also stealing signs from the town."

"We don't know that either," Oodles said. "We have no evidence."

"You're the one who went to see Sergeant Stretch to accuse him of stealing the bench across the road."

"The bench?" Moose said.

"We saw Messerschmitt sitting on the bench shortly before it disappeared," Oodles said.

"That old thing is gone?"

"I reckon the councils took it," Wish-Wash said.

"What councils?"

"Don't listen to him, Moose." Oodles straightened in his chair. "So what do they say about the leg?"

"They're operating on me first thing in the morning." Moose shook his head. "They say the X-ray shows it is broken."

"Told ya." Wish-Wash said.

Oodles blinked slowly. "Thank you, Dr Whish-Willson. Where does this leave us?"

"Up the creek without a paddle," Moose said. "As I suspected, this will put me out of action for quite some time."

He glanced up at Joffa. "So it'll be up to you to trap that Tiger. No pressure!"

"I thought you said you couldn't be sure it was a Toiger?"

"Oh, I'm sure all right. I just know better than to tell a reporter I'm sure about it until I bring it out of the bush in a cage."

Wish-Wash stood up, and the sudden movement of colour caught everyone's eyes. "I told you: I can help Joffa."

Oodles rubbed a hand across his forehead. "Not this malarkey again!"

"But now things have taken a turn for the worst, you really need me." Wish-Wash looked across at Joffa pleadingly. "You've never seen a Tiger, I have. I could be a great help."

"He has a point," Joffa said.

"Gawdsake!" Oodles said. "We're driving to Slutz Plains in the morning to get his passport sorted. All being well, we'll catch a plane to Ireland next month." He pointed to the empty bed. "If Wish-Wash is in here sharing a room with you, an awful lot of Micks are going to be disappointed about him not being there. The bush is no place for an old man."

Wish-Wash waved a fist. "I'm younger than you, remember!"

"I forgot about the foolishness of youth, then."

Moose locked his fingers and looked up at Wish-Wash. "Sit down. Oodles is right. Joffa will have to cope on his own."

Wish-Wash slumped back into his chair. "The offer stands. I'm not scared."

SIX
I SEE RED
THURSDAY MORNING.

OODLES PULLED up outside the museum at 8am sharp. He was about to turn off the engine when his peripheral vision caught the yellow-and-black hues coming his way.

Ht turned to see Wish-Wash hobbling painfully towards him.

Gawdsake! He was only wearing white shorts that looked three sizes too small, yellow-and-black striped footy socks, and a tattered Windy Mountain Tigers guernsey.

Wish-Wash pulled opened the door, and Oodles gasped: "Where on earth do you think we're going?"

"This is how I always dress when I'm going to Slutz Plains. I'm never going to let them forget we beat them in the 1994 grand final." Wish-Wash gripped the handle over the door with one hand, and lowered himself on to the red leather seat. Then he slammed the door.

"Do you have to always do that?"

"Do what?"

"Try to pull the door off its hinges."

"If you don't give these old car doors a good heave-ho, they come open."

Oodles examined Wish-Wash as he buckled his seatbelt. "Gawd-sake! It's not even blinking footy season."

"So? That means their guard will be down."

"You're not worried you might run into your ex-missus?"

Wish-Wash balled his hands into fists. "Don't start that again. You know Marta was never my missus!"

"She had your love-child."

"Will you give it a rest! You know as well as I do it was years later when I found that out."

"But she still lives in Slutz Plains, right?"

"Don't know, don't care. All I can tell you is I never see her at Billy's grave any more."

"You wouldn't see her in the dark!"

"I'd still see evidence of her. An empty gin bottle or a cigarette butt with lipstick marks."

Oodles shook his head slowly. "Do you really think anyone up there really cares about a footy game held last century?"

"Of course they flamin' do!" Wish-Wash's raised voice bounced around the cabin. "Never miss a chance to twist the knife, I say." He turned his head. "I've got some black-and-yellow streamers some-where inside so we can decorate the back of your ute if you like." He grabbed the door handle.

Oodles reached out and dragged him back. "You want to dress like a goose, that's your call. But no way are you going to make a fool out of me."

He gave Wish-Wash the once-over again. Tufts of grey chest hair protruded from the top of the guernsey. How he squeezed into those shorts was anyone's guess. He also had an odd-shaped extra bulge, which Oodles figured was a cigarette packet stuffed inside.

"Strewth! I didn't even know they made shorts like that any more," Oodles said.

"These are the original item, cobber. I keep them in the bottom of my wardrobe now I'm retired."

"You played?" Oodles drummed the steering wheel with his fingers.

"The team wasn't much chop then but the full-forward was a gun!"

"Let me guess? You were the fool-forward."

Wish-Wash sucked his stomach in and bridged high enough so he could squeeze his hand far enough into his shorts to pull out his fags. He popped one into his mouth. But his look of satisfied achievement turned to disappointment when he scanned the dashboard. "Where's your cigarette lighter gone?"

"I didn't need it any more so I replaced it with something useful. Didn't you notice I've also had the gear stick moved?" Oodles raised his voice over the throaty engine as he started off. "But I've told you before: you can't smoke in this car. It's a collector's item."

"I thought you might overlook this one little smoke for old time's sake."

"Old time's sake?"

"My old coach reckoned a smoke in the shed at half-time calmed the nerves."

"Did he? You smoking in this confined space wouldn't calm *my* nerves. Do you know how much this car is worth?" Oodles breathed out forcefully. "If you can't bear to go without a smoke on a short car trip, how are you going to go on a long airline flight?"

"I can go for a sly puff in the airplane dunny as long as you don't dob on me."

"I wouldn't have to dob you in. Those airline toilets are fitted with smoke detectors, which are hooked up to ejector toilet seats. If you don't come back to your aisle. I'll look for you out the window. '*Look, there goes Wish-Wash.*'"

Wish-Wash stuck out his bottom lip. "You think you're the only bloke who can go without a smoke! I'll get Doc Jenkins to prescribe some of those nicotine patches, and I'll pack lots of nicotine gums to chew on."

———

Oodles roared past the Sewerage Works and *The Pick of the Crop* office, which were at the foot of the 15-minute climb to Slutz Plains.

"Weren't we going to stop and pull Norm Hit's ears off?" Wish-Wash said as the car started going uphill.

Oodles's eyes didn't leave the road ahead. "He wouldn't even be at his office at this time of the morning."

"That means we'd have the element of surprise when he did arrive."

"Don't worry. We'll drop in on him on the way back." Oodles rolled up the window so he didn't get the smell of burning brakes from cars coming down the hill.

Both men stayed quiet as the car snaked around the tight bends.

Oodles finally broke the silence. "I don't know why it's even called Slutz Plains?"

"It's always been called Slutz Plains," Wish-Wash said.

"I bet the original inhabitants didn't call it that!" Oodles had to raise his voice to compete with the increasing grunt of the engine. "Plains are supposed to be flat! The Aborigines probably coined a single word for 'it's halfway up a blinking mountain'."

"I don't know what you're fretting about. Back in the day, I used to pedal my bicycle up here."

"You never!"

"I did. How else would I have got up here to the dance? It was either the bike or shank's pony."

"Is that where you met . . . ?"

Oodles didn't finish the sentence.

He came over a rise, and started slowing down as the sign told him he had arrived in Slutz Plains.

The deserted main street flattened out ahead of them, before rising again in the distance. Wish-Wash looked left and right. "Where is everyone?"

Oodles pulled his Ford Falcon ute in to a parallel parking space in front of a furniture shop.

"Do you know where the travel agency is?" Wish-Wash said.

Oodles turned and shrugged.

"Don't look at me?" Wish-Wash said. "I only ever come here to visit the op shop. I catch the bus up or Cedric brings me in his taxi and waits right outside the door." He turned around in his seat and pointed to the hall across the road. "I know that's where they used to hold the dances, but it's been converted into offices."

Oodles opened his door. "Let's go for a walk and get our bearings."

"Don't you think it's a bit cold? Slutz Plains is 1000 feet higher than Windy Mountain."

"You didn't think things through, did you? Some of us wore appropriate clothing."

"What? You think overalls are appropriate, do you? What have you comes as? A plumber?" Wish-Wash's door flew open with the same kind of force it had slammed shut.

"Which way?" Wish-Wash said as he crossed to the other side of the car, rather like a hippopotamus doing ballet with a series of tiny steps.

Oodles noticed Wish-Wash's socks were at half-mast. "Strewth! It's not like you've been running around."

Wish-Wash grinned. "It's all part of my strategy to needle them, cobber. They were probably the best-dressed team in that grand final but a fat lot of good that did them."

"What are you saying?"

"Garters are for pansies. Real men play with their socks down."

Oodles rolled his eyes. "Perhaps we *are* here too early. Maybe I should drive you home so you can to get changed."

"Don't be silly. It's not as cold as I thought it would be. I only wish I had brought a football."

Oodles looked at him.

"To have and to hold, not to kick!"

Wish-Wash walked awkwardly down the footpath. After a few steps, a box of matches fell down the back of his left leg.

He stopped, turned around, looked down and laughed. "It's not my fault these shorts haven't got pockets. You should be impressed I was able to clench the matches in my butt cheeks for so long."

Oodles rolled his eyes again. "Just don't expect *me* to pick them up!"

Wish-Wash stooped to gather the box, and as he bent over there was a loud ripping noise.

"Oh, bugger," he said as he stood up gingerly. "We'll *have* to go back now."

"Turn around, let's have a look," Oodles said.

Wish-Wash obliged and sounded like he had been shot. "It's bad, isn't it?"

"You don't look much more indecent than you already did. I'm sure we can get someone here to make running repairs. C'mon. Let's not forget what we're here for?"

They passed a variety of shops, coming to a stop outside the one whose signage declared it to be the Slutz Plains Travel Agency. The window display quoted the price of flights to the four corners of the earth, and the array of posters showed golden beaches and famous monuments.

Then Oodles pointed out another sign. "It's closed. We'll have to wait till it opens at 10."

"That's nearly two hours!"

"No, it's only 90 minutes. I thought you said you weren't cold now."

"That was before I had a new wind tunnel to contend with. Now my bum is getting numb."

"You should have thought about that."

Oodles took off down the footpath. He could hear Wish-Wash closing in on him from behind, complaining that he really needed to go home.

Then they saw the bench.

———

They only had a side view from 50 yards away. The wooden structure sat on the grassy verge between the footpath and the kerb.

Wish-Wash forgot about his wardrobe malfunction. He waggled an index finger towards the bench and his voiced strained as he spoke. "Told you they've stolen our property."

"Don't be so quick to jump to conclusions," Oodles said as they closed in. "Lots of towns have park benches where old people can sit, and they all look pretty much the same."

"I'm telling you it's our bench. I've slept on it often enough."

"Ours was a peeling, faded green. This one is a glossy, vibrant red."

"They've obviously painted it."

When they reached the bench, Oodles ran his hand along the top, and realised Wish-Wash was correct. He could feel little bumps where someone had patched all his notches with putty. The paint was still soft to the touch, and he felt dizzy.

"Are you all right?" Wish-Wash said. "I was right, wasn't I? This is our bench."

"Yes, this is the one all right." Oodles ran a hand across the top rung again, trying to regain his equilibrium.

"Didn't I tell you? Messerschmitt had nothing to do with the nicking of the bench. The two councils colluded."

Oodles started walking around the bench. It didn't make any sense, but then he spotted the plaque at the rear and he bent down and read it aloud.

DONATED BY MR M. SCHMITT

"I don't believe it," Oodles cried. "The brazen bugger is having a laugh at us now!"

Wish-Wash frowned. "I'm not with you."

"It *is* Messerschmitt, you muppet."

"You sure?"

"Have you considered both of us might be correct?" Oodles said. "That this was done by Messerschmitt working *with* the Slutz Plains Council and with the consent of Windy Mountain Council? I haven't worked out how it all fits together yet but it adds weight to your theory Messerschmitt stole those signs and I've changed my mind again about James being kidnapped. All evidence does point to Messerschmitt."

Wish-Wash shook his head. "I'll be! But what are we going to do about it?"

Oodles puffed up his cheeks. "I guess we'll have lots of time to think it through while we're sitting here waiting for the travel agency to open."

Wish-Wash slumped on to the red bench and reached for his fags again.

———

While they were sitting there, they spotted a sewing shop nearby.

Eighty minutes and four cigarettes later, it opened.

The woman who served them must have had a past life as a roadside mechanic.

She shook her head sadly when she examined Wish-Wash's burst seam, which showed off the back of his white Y-fronts.

"Beyond repair," she said. But she fitted him with three nappy clips. "They should at least get you home."

Their next stop was Oppy's fish'n'chip shop.

Proprietor Cratis Palandopolous was pleased to see Wish-Wash, which Oodles took as evidence the op shop wasn't actually the big man's only hangout in Slutz Plains.

Oppy said he hadn't turned on the deep fryer yet.

"But I'm starving," Wish-Wash said. "What else have you got to eat for breakky?"

"You ever tried a nice a Greek salad? I've got a nice a block of feta cheese and some nice a black olives." He gestured towards a table with plastic chairs and stroked his huge moustache. "Sit, sit."

———

The young travel agent looked up from the counter when they entered the shop. "How can I help you gents?"

He came around to meet them. He was the same height as Wish-Wash, and wore a name tag that pegged him as Roderick. His downy cheeks could have done with the services of a razor or even a strong wind. He was wearing green trousers and a striped black-and-white shirt.

"We was told you took passport photos here," Wish-Wash said.

"For both of you?" Roderick said.

Oodles pointed at Wish-Wash. "Just him. My passport is already sorted."

The attendant looked him up and down, probably wondering what to make of him. Wish-Wash must have looked like a broken-down old footballer who could only get sponsorship from a nappy clip manufacturer.

"Come this way." Roderick led them to a camera set up on a height-adjustable table at the side of the room. "Where are you off to?"

"Ireland," Wish-Wash said.

"Oh, you're the gentlemen that lady told me might be coming in."

"Yes, Katy McDonnell — Katy O'Fury now. You gave her a bunch of brochures," Oodles said.

"So, she's going as your carer?" Roderick said.

Wish-Wash pointed to Oodles. "No, I'm going as his carer."

Oodles shook a finger at him. "I thought we had sorted out that nonsense."

Wish-Wash ignored him and addressed the kid. "Where do you want me to stand?"

Roderick pointed out the line painted on the floor, then disappeared behind the camera.

When Wish-Wash realised the attendant was focusing on him, he broke into a big smile.

"You need to look neutral," came a disembodied voice.

"Can't I be happy our mob beat your mob?" Wish-Wash said.

Roderick's face reappeared. "Pardon?"

"In the grand final in 1994. Remember?"

"Not really. If it's any consolation, I don't remember The First Fleet flag being raised in Sydney Cove in 1788 either."

"You'll be sure to get my Windy Mountain Tigers guernsey in the shot?"

"It's a passport photo, sir. Head and shoulders. No smiling."

Wish-Wash stuck out his bottom lip. "Do you even recognise the guernsey?"

The kid's head reappeared, shaking. "No. Nana Marta might know though."

Wish-Wash spluttered. "Marta Kretocek is your grandmother?"

"You know Nana Marta?"

Wish-Wash coughed into his hand. "Used to."

"Did you know she's gone back to Poland? She was having a hard time coming to grips with dad's latest death."

———

Wish-Wash didn't say a word when the old men climbed the grand stone steps.

These were the remodelled offices at the old dance hall across the road, now owned by the Slutz Plains Council.

The steps led them into a revolving door, which deposited them into a small reception area.

"Let me handle this, I speak the council lingo," Oodles said as they stood looking around for a sign that might direct them.

"Good idea," Wish-Wash said. "I don't feel like talking anyway."

Oodles studied Wish-Wash's pale face. "Are you all right? I've never known you to be lost for words before."

"Put it down to the shock I've just had. Kids grow up so fast these days, don't they? A couple of years ago I didn't know I even had a son, now I find out I might have a grandson."

"No one ever told you?"

"Now I think back, I did see that boy at Billy's funeral. But I didn't think twice about where he fitted in."

"Have you worked out what you're going to do?" Oodles said.

"You mean: will I go back and tell him?" Wish-Wash shook his head. "No, I need time to process this."

"I wouldn't wait too long. You're looking very gaunt. I'm not sure how much longer you'll last."

This provided the jolt Wish-Wash needed. He growled. "Get away with you. You'll have to eat those words when I come to *your* funeral."

Wish-Wash blinked and looked around. "Why are we here again?"

"Strewth! Try to keep up. We're here to see Mayor Manning, to ask him what *our* park bench is doing in *his* town."

"You know him, do you?"

"Only by name. Him and James went to the same posh private boarding school. They were years apart — but I'd hazard a guess they still greet each other with secret handshakes."

Wish-Wash blinked again. "So you reckon he'll listen to us?"

"Of course he'll listen. Wouldn't you if someone was questioning the integrity of your town?"

They found the mayor's office.

Turns out, Oodles was wrong though.

Mayor Manky Manning insisted in a nasally voice that wasn't unlike the flat, robotic voice that came out of Wish-Wash's computer the red park bench had been in the Slutz Plains High Street for as long as he could remember. The donor, Mitchell Schmitt, had been one of the town's luminaries. He was long gone now, of course, but the council was doing its best to keep his memory alive. That's why the bench had just been refurbished and repainted.

He expressed sincere regret that their bench had gone missing but, really it was nothing to do with him, and if you don't mind he had a line-up of other people to see.

He herded them to the door. "I'm sorry I can't help you further. I can see you've gone to a lot of trouble dressing up to see me."

He looked Wish-Wash up and down. "I never thought I'd see that footy strip again. No wonder we beat you in two-out-of-three grand finals when you dressed like that!"

Then Wish-Wash turned and the mayor of Slutz Plains saw the nappy clips. He was guffawing when Wish-Wash slammed the door shut.

———

"Are you sure you don't want to go introduce yourself formally to your new grandson?" Oodles nodded towards the travel agency as they crossed the road on the way back to the parking spot.

Wish-Wash shook his head. "Other blokes get months of notice to get used to the idea of becoming a grandfather."

"So you need nine months to think it through?"

"I didn't say that, cobber. A few days would be nice though."

The alloy wheels glinted in the morning sun as they approached the powder-blue ute.

The street was busier now, and Oodles knew some of the passers-by were admiring his pristine machine.

The old men went to their respective sides of the car, and got in.

Wish-Wash opened the envelope containing the passport photos and examined then one by one, even though they were all the same. He turned the driver's central mirror his way and looked into it. "As I thought, he's only gone and given me a double-chin I haven't got."

Oodles swivelled the mirror back his way and wiped off Wish-Wash's fingerprints with his handkerchief. "Did you have to do that? I thought we had agreed on the need for urgency. The sooner we leave, the sooner we can tell Norm about the bench."

Wish-Wash slid the photos back into the envelope. "What makes you think Norm will even be interested by the time we finish berating him over his Tassie Tiger story?"

"He's a journo isn't he? A story is a story to someone that thick-skinned." Oodles's knuckles were white as he squeezed the steering wheel tightly. "Manning will regret brushing us off like that when he reads about it in the newspaper."

Oodles turned the key, and the ute roared into life. A few heads turned in the street, which made Oodles chuckle. Madge used to complain he used to give more attention to that ute than her, and it was true he had always incessantly polished every inch of the beast, but now no one could dissuade him whenever he wanted to make a few modifications to make the car louder and more noticeable. Most of the time he kept it locked in his garage. But every now and then he took the ute for a spin, and became the region's oldest petrol-head.

His daydream was broken by Wish-Wash. "You know what they're thinking, don't you?"

"They're probably envious."

"No, they're probably wondering how you got your hands on your son's keys."

Oodles glared sideways. "Do you want to walk home?"

"You'd leave me stranded up here?"

"You could go stay with your new grandson. I'm sure you'd have lots to catch up on."

———

Oodles turned off the engine outside the newspaper offices, and he turned to Wish-Wash. "Best to let me do most of the talking again. We don't want to blow our chances of getting something written about the bench."

Oodles looked across the dirt car park and thought about what he was going to say.

When they climbed the external metal stairs and entered the cavernous office, Norm was tapping away on his computer.

Wish-Wash stormed across the room. "We've got a bone to pick with you, Shit."

Norm stopped typing and looked up. "It's Hit, actually. I thought you knew what my surname was?" Then he looked even more surprised. "Why are you dressed like that, Wish-Wash? It's not even footy season."

Oodles pinched an eyebrow. Trust Wish-Wash to suddenly find his booming voice! "We've just been up to Slutz Plains."

Norm looked at him blankly. "Oh, that explains it then!"

"Never mind what I'm wearing," Wish-Wash said. "Didn't they rename you Shit when they moved the newspaper office out here next to the sewerage works?"

Norm bounced up. "Look, I didn't have any say in moving to this place. When they mentioned at my interview they were looking for more appropriate premises, I told them it didn't matter to me where I worked as long as I could plug in my laptop." He pulled a face. "I probably should have clarified it a bit. You know this warehouse used to be an abattoir? I swear I can hear ghostly moos coming from downstairs sometimes."

Wish-Wash prodded him on the chest. "Why did you have to go write we're on the verge of catching a Tasmanian Tiger?"

"That's just what the Irishman told me."

"That's not what Joffa says. He says he barely mentioned that. He thought you wanted to know about how Moose came to break his leg."

"That's correct. I did. But I got a better story. I thought you — of all people — would have been pleased."

"Me?"

"Everyone knows you're one of the *I-saw-a-Tasmanian-Tiger* pioneers."

Wish-Wash looked stunned. "I get it. You don't believe me, do you?"

"It doesn't matter what I believe. Tasmanian Tiger sightings have always made good copy. Readers don't care if the publications don't come up with proof."

Oodles raked his hair with his fingers. "Even if Joffa did say that, and I'm not saying he did, should you be taking much heed of a foreigner who has lived in the city most of his life and probably doesn't know the difference between a Tasmanian Devil and a Tasmanian Tiger?"

"It's not my job to analyse, just to report."

"Isn't that just irresponsible journalism?"

Norm shrugged. "If we waited until everything was proved conclusively, we'd never get a single paper out."

"How come then you didn't write a word about Jimbo being kidnapped?" Wish-Wash said.

"We do have *some* standards and legal constraints," Norm said.

"But the Tassie Tiger is fair game because it sells papers?" Oodles said.

"Look at it from my point of view. The print newspaper used to be a hungry beast. But you'd have time to breathe once you filled your 24 pages or 36 pages. The online edition never sleeps. The deadlines just keep coming. The unlimited space can never actually be filled. And what can I say about the new owners? You give them more, and they want more . . . and more . . . and more."

"Where do your standards and legal obligations stand on the park bench?" Oodles said.

"What park bench?"

"The one in our main street that's been nicked. Wish-Wash and I have just seen it in the main street of Slutz Plains."

Norm rubbed the back of his neck. "I didn't even know it was missing. Are you sure it's the same one?"

"I ought to know it's ours. They did a pretty good job filling in all the holes I made, but it's like Braille to me."

Wish-Wash spluttered. "What's even worse is the Slutz Plains mayor gave us the brush-off as if we were two doddery old fools! He says it's their bench, and it's been at that spot for yonks."

"What does Sergeant Stretch say?"

Oodles shook his head. "We haven't seen him yet. Has he made any progress on the disappearing signs?"

"Not that I've heard," Norm said.

"Mark my words," Wish-Wash said. "Messerschmitt is as guilty as sin, and when Stretch joins the dots, he'll solve the kidnap riddle too. But Messerschmitt has made his first mistake. He only realised after he nicked the sign outside the rose garden that he didn't need any of those letters, so he discarded it in a place few people would look."

Norm looked puzzled. "Where?"

Wish-Wash gave him a hard look. "Don't tell me you haven't seen it?"

"No. Where?"

"Unbelievable," Wish-Wash said. "It's only been up on the fence next door since yesterday. You seriously haven't seen it?"

"Why would even look? The pong can be brutal out there. I park the car as near to this building as I can, and I don't hang around at the end of the day either if I can help it."

Wish-Wash smiled for the first time. "This is your lucky day, then. You'll be able to go to the scene of the crime and photograph it."

Norm looked at his shoes. "In the good old days, we had actual photographers," he mumbled.

"It's a vital piece of evidence you're going to need to photograph if you're going to pursue the case of the stolen bench."

"There is a link?" Norm looked up, even more surprised. "I thought you are accusing Messerschmitt of stealing the signs, and the Slutz Plains Council of stealing the bench. Aren't they two different crimes?"

"We now think Messerschmitt and the Slutz Plains Council may have joined forces," Oodles said.

The room fell silent.

Oodles could see Norm was trying to process this new theory, and he threw him another googly. "Do you still have a hatch, match and despatch column now you're online?"

Norm nodded slowly, trying to work out what was coming next.

"I think Wish-Wash wants to welcome his new grandson into the world."

———

"That flamin' reporter has put us in a terrible situation." Wish-Wash just got the words out before he opened the door of the museum. But he froze, which caused Oodles to run into him.

"Now what?" Oodles said. "Why have you stopped?"

Wish-Wash turned. "He's smiling," he whispered.

"Smiling?" Oodles looked under Wish-Wash's armpit and saw Awesome Sauce grinning at them from behind the reception desk.

"Wish-Wash, Oodles, welcome back," came the twang. "How was your visit to Slutz Plains?"

Oodles poked Wish-Wash gently in the ribs. "See, he's just happy to see us. C'mon, get a move on."

Wish-Wash stumbled forward, and he triggered the door bell, which started playing the theme music to *Skippy, the Bush Kangaroo*.

"I knew it." Wish-Wash looked back angrily at the box above the door, oblivious that yet another person could see his nappy clips. "What in God's name is this supposed to be?"

"You don't know?" Awesome Sauce said.

"Oh, I know, all right. But this is the Windy Mountain *Tasmanian Tiger* Museum, not the flamin' Windy Mountain *Kangaroo* Museum. You'll turn us into a laughing stock."

"I thought you said the Tiger was a marsupial with more in common with Skippy than a Bengal Tiger or a Snow Leopard?"

"What was wrong with the door bell the way it was? People are comfortable enough with ding-dong."

"You know if granddaddy had got his way with the theme park idea, his rides would have growled. He knew the value of a bit of theatre. Nice diaper clips, by the way."

Wish-Wash put his hands on his hips. "So the truth emerges! You *are* some kind of a spy for your grandfather." He looked around the room suspiciously. "Have you bugged this place? Is someone listening into us?"

"That's a ridiculous accusation," the American kid said. "I told you. I'm here on a backpacking holiday. Granddaddy gave up on buying this place years ago."

"That's good news because you tell him it's still not for sale." Wish-Wash looked up at the box above the door and repeated it in case eavesdroppers were listening. "DID YOU HEAR THAT? THE TASMANIAN TIGER MUSEUM IS STILL *NOT* FOR SALE." He turned. "Is it, Oodles?"

Oodles shrugged. "For the right price maybe?"

Wish-Wash's eyes narrowed. "What are you saying? We can't sell when we're on the verge of finding a live Tasmanian Tiger!"

"You said it yourself," Oodles said. "*The Pick of the Crop* report has buggered up all that. And with Moose out of action, we have no hope of even catching it."

"I told you, I can help Joffa," Wish-Wash said.

"How many times do I have to say no?" Oodles shouted. "I don't need you coming out of the bush on a stretcher. You're not going, and that's that." He lowered his voice. "I didn't think I'd miss James, but I do, and I know I'd miss you twice as much."

"You mean that?"

"Gawdsake! Don't make me say it again."

Awesome Sauce continued as if he had never been admonished. "So, how did Slutz Plains go? Did you get your passport photos?"

"Wish-Wash saw his grandson," Oodles said.

"See him often, do you?" Awesome Sauce said to Wish-Wash.

"He's *never* seen him before," Oodles said.

The young Texan looked at Wish-Wash blankly.

"We also saw our bench," Oodles said. "It's been reassembled in the main street of Slutz Plains."

"Don't all park benches look much the same?" Awesome Sauce said.

Oodles shook his head. "I'd know that bench anywhere. You can fill in the lumps and bumps with putty, but you can't disguise its personality. We've put Norm Hit on the case."

Awesome Sauce gave him a puzzled look. "Who's he?"

"He's the journalist who reported Joffa said we're on the verge of catching a Tasmanian Tiger." He turned to Wish-Wash. "Thanks to that story, we will have every man and his dog combing Bing Bong Mountain trying to beat us to the punch. I wouldn't be surprised to hear that Messerschmitt and his German shepherd are up there."

"Messerschmitt?" Awesome Sauce said.

"He's our chief suspect for everything bad happening around here," Oodles said.

Wish-Wash glared at the young Texan. "The only thing we don't like him for is the sabotage of the flamin' door bell."

"Will you get off Awesome Sauce's case!" Oodles said. "We need to work out what on earth are we going to do about trapping this Tasmanian Tiger now Moose is out of action?"

"I could help Joffa."

Oodles and Wish-Wash's eyes zeroed in on Awesome Sauce.

"You've only been here five minutes!" Wish-Wash cried.

"This is my third day, actually. How HARD could it be?"

Wish-Wash pointed to the wall to their left. "Do you know how dangerous it is out there?"

Awesome Sauce frowned. "At the shopping centre?"

Realising his mistake, Wish-Wash pivoted and pointed to another wall in the direction of Bing Bong Mountain. "Do you know how many years Moose has been looking for the Tasmanian Tiger? Even though he knows every blade of grass on that mountain, look where he is now?"

"You don't think he's getting old and careless?"

"Wash your mouth out, boy!" Wish-Wash said. "I wouldn't let Moose hear you calling him old!"

Oodles nodded, but then he said, "It might work though." He caught Wish-Wash's eye. "It's certainly a better solution than you going bush."

"You reckon?" Wish-Wash said.

"And it'd get him out of your hair." He turned to Awesome Sauce. "No offence, but you're likely to do him in if you keep changing his door bell."

Far from looking offended, the American grabbed this as a further selling point. "Oodles is right. I can't tinker if I'm not here."

Wish-Wash shook his head. "I don't know. Joffa is pretty green himself."

"I'm eager to learn." Awesome Sauce looked from face to face. "What do you say?"

Oodles searched Wish-Wash's eyes. "I really think Awesome Sauce is worth a shot."

Wish-Wash pinched the bridge of his nose, then sighed. "I'll talk to Joffa, see what he says." He headed to the stairs to go change. He turned and waved a finger at the Yank. "But if I find out this is one of your grandfather's little tricks to buy this place cheaply, I'll tell Joffa to leave you lost up there."

SEVEN
SWEET DREAMS ARE MADE OF CHEESE

OODLES OUGHT to have known he was dreaming. His ute had turned emerald green, and he was lost in the dark, icy mountains of County Donegal.

His windscreen wipers were swishing furiously when he pulled up outside a stone house.

The old men had wasted the whole day trying to locate Wish-Wash's ancestral home, and they had decided in desperation they needed to find someone to give them directions before everyone had gone to bed.

Oodles couldn't be sure they were even in the right part of the county. They hadn't even seen a town sign in the dark, though this looked like at least a village.

Wish-Wash squinted out the rain-splattered windows. "Where is everyone?"

Oodles nodded towards one of the chimneys, which was shooting out pale, grey smoke and orange embers. "My guess is they are all inside keeping warm."

"You don't think Messerschmitt got here before us and nicked the town sign?" Wish-Wash said.

Oodles glared at him. "What? You reckon he's inside one of those toasty-warm cottages getting ready to assemble his ransom note?"

"Why are you always ridiculing my ideas?" Wish-Wash said. "I thought we were partners?"

"I'll tell you what we are. We're fucked and a long way from home."

That's another moment Oodles ought to have realised he was deep in the REM stage of sleep. He never swore. Not really. The occasional 'bugger', and 'Gawdsake' were the worst words in his vocabulary. The f-word had never passed his lips. What's more, he had never been to Ireland and ought to have no idea what a village in Donegal looked like?

The dream just got weirder.

Oodles switched off the engine. "We'll just have to knock on some doors. You take this side, I'll do the other side."

When he got out, the rain stopped. This was even more evidence he was dreaming because Joffa had told him the rain rarely stopped in Ireland, even on the grandest of days.

The first thing he saw in the glow of a street light was a freshly-painted green park bench across the road.

"I'll be buggered, it's our bench." He walked over and ran his hand over the top to sweep away the beads of rainwater. He could feel where the putty had filled in all the ruts he had made.

"You're spot on, this is *our* bench," came a voice from behind.

Oodles looked around, expecting to see Wish-Wash. But instead he was surprised.

"James! What are you doing here?"

"Wish-Wash invited me, remember?" His warm breath made a speech bubble as it hit the cold air. "I demand thee pray tell me who's been cocking his leg on mine great, great, great grandfather's statue each morning."

Oodles arched his eyebrows. "How do you know about that?"

"I'm the Mayor. It's my job to knoweth."

Oodles rubbed his freezing hands together as he pondered what to say. "I'm sorry, James. But you must realise you haven't been mayor for some years?" He was about to elaborate but he heard footsteps behind him and turned his head to investigate. No one was there. Odd! He turned back and James had also vanished. The only thing in the vicinity was the bench. "Gawdsake!"

"Are you talking to yourself?" another voice said. When Oodles turned again, Wish-Wash was breathing out streams of hot air.

Oodles put a hand to his chest. "Since when has a clodhopper like you been able to sneak up on anyone?"

"I've been knocking on doors, OK? I thought this bloke could help us."

"What bloke?"

A balding man with long, straggly hair stepped into the light. Oodles had seen *The Rocky Horror Picture Show* with Madge in 1977. This is why he should not have been surprised when Riff-Raff took him by the hand and familiar music started. Dozens of people emerged from the cottages and started dancing the *Time Warp* in the street.

What was even weirder was he knew some of the people.

Joffa was dancing with Katy.

Madge waved at him from the shadows and mouthed some words. He couldn't hear her above the music. He just knew the words were *Bon Voyage.*

Oodles saw three other people he knew sitting on the bench. Mayor Manky Manning was wearing fishnet stockings and imparting instructions to the dancers. On either side of him were Moose Routley, whose left leg was in a plaster cast, and a gangly kid wearing green trousers and a striped black-and-white shirt with a badge that named him as Roderick.

Be buggered if Messerschmitt wasn't in the middle of the road too, dancing with his German shepherd.

Awesome Sauce was dancing with a Rupert Bear stunt-double, who was wearing a cowboy hat.

Norm Hit was dancing with a manual typewriter, which was floating in the air.

As Oodles twirled, he caught the bench in his corner of his eye again. He came to a standstill when he realised Mayor Manning, Moose and Roderick were no longer sitting on it.

Someone else was lying face-down on the structure. The music morphed into a funeral hymn.

Oodles couldn't see the face of the supine figure because he was obscured by a priest in black robes.

But one look at the yellow happy pants told him all he had to know.

"Nooooo," he cried, as he ran towards them. This ought to have been yet another clue he was dreaming! Oodles hadn't been able to run for years. But this time he sprinted as if he were 13 years old.

Father O'Boring put his hand out to stop him, and smiled. "Dat poor old fella has smoked his last fag. I'm just giving him da Last Rites." He tapped the wood above Wish-Wash's head and muttered some words that might have been Latin or might have been some Irish mumbo-jumbo.

Knock-knock, knock-knock.

Oodles woke up.

His sweaty pyjama top was sticking to him again.

Knock-knock, knock-knock.

Someone was at the door.

Oodles looked at his watch. It was 9.30am! He didn't normally sleep this late!

He rolled out of bed and grabbed his dressing gown from a bed knob.

He suspected when he opened the front door he'd probably look as if he had just seen a ghost.

But he was wrong.

Wish-Wash was the one who looked more like he had seen a ghost.

———

"Thank Christ, you're not dead." Wish-Wash looked at him with tear-filled eyes.

Oodles swallowed and stepped aside. "You'd better come in."

Wish-Wash went past in a kaleidoscope of red, blue and lime green, and made a beeline for the living room where he sat down on the other side of the table.

"*The Pick of the Crop* says we were both killed in a car accident last night," he blurted.

Oodles stood with his hands on his hips on the other side of the table. "It says *what*?"

"Awesome Sauce helped me get on to the site again because I wanted to see what Norm had written about the bench. Imagine my shock when I read the main headline: TOWN'S OLDEST HOON AND HIS SIDEKICK KILLED IN CRASH."

Oodles slumped into the nearest chair. "Why would Norm write such a thing?"

Wish-Wash shook his head. "The story quotes a Sergeant Schultz."

Oodles drummed his fingers on the table. "Never heard of him."

Wish-Wash's bottom lip protruded as he looked around the room. "What have you done with the rest of the Iced Vo-Vo's?"

"How can you think about biscuits at a time like this? I thought you didn't like them anyway?"

"I've had a great shock. It's not every day you read about your own death?"

Oodles got up and went into the kitchen to fill the jug.

When he returned, Wish-Wash spluttered: "The story said we had crashed into the statue of Colonel Northan."

Oodles's eyes narrowed and he raised his voice as the noise from the jug rose in the adjoining room. "Gawdsake!"

"I wondered if it was a case of mistaken identity. Perhaps you had found Jimbo and he was your passenger, not me?"

Oodles rolled his eyes. "How could you possibly think that?"

"I didn't feel like I was dead."

Oodles returned to the kitchen and came back with a tray containing the teapot, two mugs, a milk jug, a sugar bowl and an already opened packet of biscuits, which he transferred on to the yellow tabletop. "Surely, you only had to go outside and look down the street to reassure yourself the statue was still in one piece!"

"Matter of fact, that's exactly what I did." Wish-Wash grabbed for the packet and extracted a biscuit.

"But you still thought Jimbo and I still might have bought it?"

Wish-Wash shoved his Iced Vo-Vo into his mouth, chewed hastily and swallowed. "I figured if this Sergeant Schultz could get our identities wrong, he might have also mixed up his statues."

"Windy Mountain has only got one statue."

Wish-Wash shrugged as he picked up the teapot and started pouring. "Who knows? Perhaps he got mixed up with statue in another town? How am I to know where you might have found Jimbo? The more I thought about it, the more I dismissed it as another one of Norm's porky pies. But I got worried again when you didn't walk by with Gough this morning. That's why I'm here."

Oodles shook his head as he sat back down. He watched Wish-Wash shovel four spoons of sugar into his mug.

"I *did* find James in an unlikely place last night, as it happens." Oodles said.

"You did find him? Where?"

"In Donegal."

"Donegal? That's crazy! He wouldn't be seen dead in Ireland."

"Oh, he was very much alive; you were the one who didn't look too well."

"Are you on drugs!"

"No, but I think I might have been under the influence. Cheese always makes my dreams vivid. I knew I shouldn't have eaten so much feta at Oppy's yesterday."

Wish-Wash stared at him. "And you dreamed Jimbo was with us in Ireland? That would never happen."

Oodles started sipping his tea. "James wasn't the only one. Madge was there, as I'd expect; Joffa and Katy were there too; even Messerschmitt was there with his dog; and your grandson made an appearance. Who else? Moose. Awesome Sauce. Possibly his grandfather. Riff-Raff. Mayor Manning was wearing fishnet stockings and we were all doing the *Time Warp*."

"Who's Riff-Raff?"

"You must know him? He's the creepy bloke from *The Rocky Horror Picture Show*."

Wish-Wash helped himself to another biscuit. "And I was doing the flamin' *Time Warp*?"

"No, you were lying dead on our bench. Did I mention some village in Donegal has nicked our bench now? Father O'Boring was giving you the Last Rites."

Wish-Wash rolled his eyes. "Not this again!"

"It might not have been all the fault of the cheese," Oodles said. "I popped a sleeping tablet last night. With everything that happened yesterday, I knew I'd have trouble sleeping. Not that it worked very well. I tossed and turned for ages before I went to sleep."

Wish-Wash reached in for another Iced Vo-Vo, held it up and examined it. "I really thought I'd never see these biscuits again."

Oodles scowled. "I think we ought to go see Norm and ask him what the dickens he thinks he's doing this time."

"It'll have to wait." Wish-Wash looked to the clock on the wall and wiped pink crumbs from his mouth. "I've arranged to meet Katy at the cafe at 11, so I can hand those passport forms and photos over. We'll have to stay for a cuppa and a biscuit because it's the polite thing to do."

Oodles tapped his forehead. "I've got my checkup with Doc Jenkins at noon. I can't miss that! Not if you want me on that plane."

Wish-Wash rapped a finger on the table. "I thought you had decided to bypass that quack?"

"No, that was *your* idea. Doc Jenkins has kept me relatively healthy all these years."

"He didn't even tell you to stay off the mind-altering cheese! You have to question his competence even if he does tick you off for the trip to Ireland." Wish-Wash slurped the last of his tea.

"I can't see why he wouldn't give me the all clear?" Oodles said. "If he's read today's paper, he's going to think I'm the healthiest dead bloke in Windy Mountain."

———

When the old men broke through the curtains, the first person they saw was Wendy cleaning a table with a cloth. She looked up at them. "Speak of the devils!"

She turned to a puffy-eyed Katy, who was seated at the other table. "I told you they couldn't be dead."

Wish Wash pulled out the chair opposite Katy and passed over the envelope containing the passport photos and his application.

Oodles sat down beside him. "Don't tell me you believed that malarkey in *The Pick of the Crop*, sweetie?"

"Honestly, Oodles?" Katy clutched the envelope to her chest. "I didn't know what to think. I don't even normally read the news online but Tim Noah showed us how to get around the firewall for free."

"Awesome Sauce?" Wish-Wash spluttered.

"Yes, he came around last night."

Wish-Wash closed his eyes slowly. "Why would that know-all even go to your flat? I haven't even had a chance to talk to Joffa yet."

"Now you don't have to. Tim said you had agreed to let him team up with Joffa, and he wanted to know if Joffa was OK with that. I guess him showing us how to bypass the firewall was his way of getting him onside."

Oodles stopped fidgeting with the sugar bowl and looked up. "So, what did you think when you saw the report about our deaths?"

"How do you think I felt? I was devastated I hadn't had the chance to say goodbye."

Oodles held her gaze. "When did you start having second thoughts?"

"Joffa said he hadn't heard any commotion in the High Street, so he stuck his head out the window and saw the statue was in one piece."

Wish-Wash started laughing like a donkey. The escalating rumble developed into a coughing fit, and Oodles stood up and thumped him between the shoulder blades. "Cough it up, Eeyore. It might be a gold watch."

Wendy looked down at Katy again. "I told you they'd be in, love, didn't I? They wouldn't miss morning tea on the house." She disappeared out the back.

Katy watched the saloon door swing back and forwards. She looked at Oodles, who had taken his seat again.

"When I raised the possibility you might actually have crashed up at Slutz Plains, and *The Pick of the Crop* had got some of its facts wrong, Wendy said no way would someone with your driving skills run into a stationary statue . . . unless you looked up and saw James Northan's severed head on top of it."

"She said that?" Oodles puffed out his chest with pride, but then he processed what she had said. "Now, that's not funny. We still can't find him anywhere."

Wish-Wash's watery eyes brightened. "We haven't looked up there though!"

"Will you cut it out?" Oodles said. "James might not be the most popular kid on the block, but he's part of the fabric of this town, he's missing and he deserves a bit of respect."

The room fell silent. The next noise they heard was the kitchen door swinging open and Wendy emerging holding a tray.

She put the tray down on the table. "Why the long faces? This is a celebration. Free tea and biscuits for my two best customers." She glanced across at Katy. "And for you too, love."

Katy smiled, and Wendy turned and went back to the kitchen.

Katy opened the envelope, and examined the contents with a poker-face as if she were sifting through a small pack of cards.

"Like the photos?" Oodles said. "His grandson took them."

Katy looked up sharply. "I didn't know you had a grandson, Wish-Wash?"

"Neither did he," Oodles said.

Wish-Wash loosened his tie. "Will you give it a rest, Oodles. We don't have conclusive proof."

"That's what you said about Billy Gumboots until it was too late," Oodles said.

Katy looked from face to face. "I didn't know Billy was even married? And he had a kid? He hid that well."

"Family tradition," Oodles said.

Wish-Wash waved a fist at Oodles. "It's a good thing you have an appointment with the doctor soon. You can ask him to fix your broken nose."

"Are you threatening me? You know what happened last time we had fisticuffs."

Katy called out loudly. "Gentlemen, please!"

Wish-Wash reached for the teapot. "Shall I be mother?" he said, sighing.

"Be anything you like," Oodles said. "I just know if I had potential off-spring I'd move heaven and earth to get some proof."

"How do you know you don't have a little bastard somewhere?" Wish-Wash said.

"Unlike you, I never played away from home."

"I never had a home to play away from." He held up a single finger. "What happened, happened once. ONCE. A knee-trembler behind the bike shed after the dance."

Katy held up her hands. "Too much information, Wish-Wash. Ewww."

Oodles shook his head. "If a DNA test can prove you're related to someone in Donegal, it must be able to work out dead cert if you're related to a kid in Slutz Plains. Don't you think you owe it to him, after what you never did for Billy?"

Wish-Wash slid the cups over. "Let's change the subject, shall we?"

He looked across at Katy. "I would have thought the fact we found *our* park bench reassembled on the main street of Slutz Plains would be much more interesting than my private life."

Katy searched Oodles's eyes for confirmation.

Oodles nodded. "We went to see Mayor Manning but I should have known he has no intention of listening to anyone who can't vote for him."

Katy drained her tea as she examined Wish-Wash's passport application to make sure it was all in order and he had certified the photos. "I have to go. I'll counter-sign these photos and get everything in the post today. I'll leave you two sleuths with it."

———

Norm stopped typing and looked up when the old men burst through the door.

Then he turned white. "How? . . . what? . . . not possible."

"Will you stop jibbering?" Oodles stormed over to his desk, which was underneath a wall clock that said it was 2.30pm.

"But you're d-d-dead!"

"Do we look dead to you?" Oodles tapped Norm's face with a cuffed hand. "Do I feel cold like a blinking ghost?"

Norm kept staring at him. "But Sergeant Schultz said you were both killed when you crashed into the statue!"

Oodles scoffed. "Didn't you think it was strange it was still standing when you drove past it this morning on your way to work?"

Norm shook his head. "I couldn't bear to look at the crash scene, so I drove here by the backroads, past Jobson's Farm."

Wish-Wash stepped forward. "Who is this Sergeant Shultz anyway?"

Norm got to his feet shakily. "I've never met him. But he called up last night just before I was about to knock off and told me the whole, horrible story."

"And you believed him?"

"Why wouldn't I believe him?" Norm returned his glare. "He said he was filling in for Sergeant Stretch."

"Gawdsake!" Oodles said. "Didn't you do your cadetship under Dobber Leggs? Surely he taught you about verifying sources and cross-checking facts?"

"It was easier for him in those days. You only had to stick your head out the window to see what was happening in the town."

"You could have phoned someone?" Oodles hissed.

"Who would I phone at that time of night?"

"Aren't reporters supposed to be ultra-sceptical? Didn't you even wonder about this Sergeant Shultz being who he said he was?"

"Why would I? He sounded like any other copper, just one with a heavy German accent."

Wish-Wash and Oodles looked at each other. "He was a Kraut?" Oodles said.

Norm nodded. "He even said 'ja vol'."

"Ja vol?" Oodles flipped his head upwards. "Don't Germans only utter that in the movies!"

"Say?" Wish-Wash said. "You don't think it was actually Messer-schmitt pretending to be a cop?"

Oodles looked him in the eye. "You know as well as I do Messer-schmitt is not German."

"His dog is."

"Great, we'll go with your talking dog theory, shall we?" Oodles turned back to Norm. "Ignore this muppet! What exactly did this so-called copper say?"

"I told you, he had the police-speak down pat, that's how I knew he was ridgy-didge. Who else but German coppers say things like, 'At approximately 9.16 in the evening, ja vol, a motor vehicle driven by Clarence John Noodle came in collision with a statue in the High Street, ja vol. As a result, Mr Noodle is now incinerated, believed deceased, ja vol, as is his passenger, Bertram Barry Whish-Willson and the statue depicting the previously already-deceased Colonel Richard Northan, ja vol.'"

Oodles looked back at Wish-Wash. "You never told me your middle name was Barry?"

"Who says it is? You believe this Sergeant Shultz too?"

"At least he got my names right." Oodles stood thinking. "Oh, and I forgot to tell you. Doc Jenkins has given me the green light." He coughed nervously. "With one little caveat."

————

Oodles was feeling guilty when he finally hit the High Street with Gough about 4pm.

It wasn't the dog's fault Oodles had slept in and had then been kept busy meeting various appointments.

Gough wagged his tail all the way into town.

It was Oodles who went all pale when he looked up before crossing over to the statue.

Messerschmitt was standing by like a proud father as his German shepherd squatted at the base of the statue!

"What the . . ?" Oodles mumbled as he watched Messerschmitt's dog defecate on one of the horse's hind legs.

Gough barked his encouragement, and the yelp made Messerschmitt turn and smile.

Oodles turned around when he heard a swishing noise.

Wendy had emerged through the bead curtains to do her afternoon outside clean-up outside the Wind Tunnel Cafe.

She leaned on her broom and nodded towards Messerschmitt. "Glad you're another witness, love. This has become his daily ritual of defiance."

She sucked up her breath noisily. "I don't know what anyone ever saw in that ratbag? He hasn't got a job, he spends way too much time in the pub, he damn-well encourages that big dog of his to foul the statue every day at this time, and no one in this town is man enough to say boo to him."

Oodles spluttered: "Don't expect me to set an example."

"No one expects you to take him to task, love, but you'd think the council would put a stop to it."

It was a good point. Oodles knew that statue brought tourists to the town. Coffs Harbour had its Big Banana, Nambour had its Big Pineapple, Goulburn had its Big Merino and Windy Mountain had its Big Doofus.

Wendy began sweeping but stopped abruptly. "Will you look at that. Some dirty bugger has spat on my bit of the footpath." She sneered at Messerschmitt over the road. "Bet your life it was him."

She sighed. "You just wait and see. No one will dare try to stop him, but you can bet your bottom dollar they're over in the Council Chambers watching him through the windows right now. Soon as he goes, some poor junior will come out with a plastic bag and a bucket of water with a scrubbing brush, and clean up the mess."

"They're watching? Really?" Oodles looked down at Gough. "Let's say we give the statue a miss today, boy."

As they crossed the road and passed Messerschmitt and his dog, the man with the wild hair smiled. "O'right, Oodles?"

———

Oodles tore at his receding hair as he stood outside the museum and squinted towards the statue. A tiny figure with a bucket knelt at the base.

Wish-Wash bent down behind him and patted Gough, who was tied up to a post by the footpath.

"We skipped the park," Oodles said. "I wanted to get out of Messerschmitt's orbit as soon as possible, especially when he addressed me by name. How does he even know that? I've never even met him."

"Keep your hair on! It's pretty hard to be anonymous in a town of this size!"

"But he *knows* my name!"

"So? He probably asked someone. *Who's that decrepit old man?*"

Oodles stared at Wish-Wash darkly. "Doc Jenkins reckons if I was any fitter, I'd be dangerous."

"And you believed him? The man is incompetent. He told me I'm the perfect weight for someone who's six foot eight. But if he had bothered to check his records he would have seen I'm only six foot one."

"You know what else he did?"

"Jenko?"

"No, Messerschmitt!"

"What?"

"He smiled at me."

Wish-Wash's eyes widened. "He *smiled* at you?" He stretched the word out.

"You didn't see it. It was a taunting smile."

"Taunting?"

"It was a smile that also had guilt written all over it. *I kidnapped James, but you can't prove it.*"

"Where do you think he's hiding Jimbo, then?" Wish-Wash said. "Somewhere near the tip? In the bush? If he's holding him in that one-bedroom cottage of his, why hasn't someone reported hearing something?"

"It's pretty hard to tap out S.O.S. in Morse code when your hands are bound," Oodles said.

"Why hasn't he yelled out then?"

"He must be gagged."

The old men watched the distant person with the bucket stand up and cross back over to the council chambers.

Wish-Wash scratched his head. "What do we really know about Messerschmitt? We don't even know his real name. How's that going to look if he gets his name on the honour board in the pub as the new drunk?"

Oodles held his gaze. "Is that even likely? He's only lived in the town for a blink of the eye. It'd be breaking with tradition to appoint an outsider."

"Tradition doesn't matter a lot to this younger generation," Wish-Wash said. "My intel is that Barely Legal Leigh plans to quit the job because he's landed himself an apprenticeship as a boilermaker — and someone has to fill the void."

Oodles scrunched his eyes shut. "The paint couldn't have dried on Leigh's name."

Wish-Wash rubbed the back of his neck. "The real shame is no other person on that board has had a police record against their name."

"What about drunk and disorderly?"

"That's different." Wish-Wash said. "That's an occupational hazard. But murder is in another league."

"Who's Messerschmitt murdered?"

"It's obvious, isn't it? He *must* be Sergeant Shultz! He killed us off in the newspaper, didn't he? No telling what he might do to Jimbo if his family can't come up with the money."

———

Saturday morning

Oodles watched Gough spray the horse's hind legs.

He was compelled to watch because every time he closed his eyes, two images burned into his brain. One was of James's severed head speared on top of the statue, the other was Messerschmitt's German shepherd defecating on the base.

When the horse's legs were wet with pee, they crossed to the park where Gough continued his crime spree.

Then they headed back down the High Street towards the museum.

As Oodles approached, he saw unfamiliar vehicles parked outside. Gawdsake! What was going on?

The biggest vehicle was an orange crane and the other two were white dual-cab utes.

When he came closer, he could see people wearing hard hats were inside the vehicles. They stared back at him with expressions that suggested they might have eaten broken glass for breakfast.

The doors of the utes were emblazoned with the logo of 'Jonno's Rleocation Service'.

Through the museum window he could see Wish-Wash standing in the foyer waving his arms at a large man wearing an orange safety vest.

Oodles tied up Gough and headed inside.

The door played *Jingle Bells* as he entered, even though it was January. Awesome Sauce was sitting on the other side of the reception desk staring bewilderedly at the computer as the muscle-bound man argued with Wish-Wash.

"What in the blazes is going on?" Oodles said.

Wish-Wash pointed a shaking finger at Orange Man, who was wearing a sleeveless shirt that showed off his tattoo-covered biceps. "This Scottish git says he has an order to demolish this building."

Oodles addressed the stranger. "Surely you have the wrong address?"

"No, pal." The man stooped down and put his white hard-hat on the floor, then he raised his clipboard to the counter and opened it. Oodles sidled up beside him and craned his head. "See, the Windy Mountain Tasmanian Tiger Museum."

Oodles smiled politely. "This must be some kind of mistake."

"No mistake, pal, see." Oodles realised Orange Man had two missing front teeth. "It's signed by the museum's owner."

He stabbed at the clipboard again, and Oodles leaned in.

"B, Whish-Willson, see."

Oodles looked up at Wish-Wash, seeking explanation.

"Let me see that?" Wish-Wash wrenched the clipboard out of Toothless Orange Man's hands and examined it.

"This isn't my signature." He frowned at Oodles. "I would never order the demolition of this place, you know that?"

"Who said anything aboot demolition?" Toothless Orange Man said. "We've been hired to relocate this museum to Slutz Plains. If we just had to demolish the place we'd only need two men and a wrecking ball." He pointed out the window. "We wouldn't need all those fellas and equipment."

Oodles rubbed the back of his neck. "Where's this document even come from?"

Toothless Orange Man shrugged. "The boss faxed it to me last night."

"The boss?"

"Jonny."

"I think I need to phone him to sort this out," Oodles said. "Someone has obviously sent him a forged signature."

"I haven't got the time for this, yer know." Toothless Orange Man folded his arms and looked down at Oodles.

"Look, I'm sure this can be sorted out." Oodles reached for the black phone on the counter. "What's Jonny's last name?"

Toothless Orange Man shrugged. "I don't know. I've never met him."

"You've never met your boss?"

"He faxes me the assignments."

"Where's he based?"

Toothless Orange Man shrugged.

"Doesn't he speak to you on the phone?"

Toothless Orange Man shook his head. "I told you: he faxes me. As long as the jobs get done, my bank account keeps going ca-ching, ca-ching."

"And you don't think that's odd?"

"I've never really thought aboot it." He looked from Oodles's face to Wish-Wash's to Awesome Sauce's. "You shouldn't either, not if you know what's good for you." He pointed outside again. "Those other six fellas are just as eager to get to work as me, only I think yer'll find they're not as polite as me." He smirked. "Understand?"

Oodles and Wish-Wash looked at each other, considering their options.

Where was Moose when you needed him?

This bloke, as big and ugly as he was, wouldn't even dare try to intimidate him!

Toothless Orange Man must have read their minds. "Oh, I nearly forgot to say. Jonny sends get-well-quick greetings to Moose." He smirked again as he bent forward and looked over to the other side of the counter. "I take it he's not hiding, is he?"

If he hadn't had his back to the door, he would have noticed Joffa coming through the entrance.

It was only the sound of *Jingle Bells* that made him turn, and that's when he saw the six-foot-six man-mountain waving his fist at the box above the door.

"What the feck? Christmas music! Really?" Joffa turned and glared at Toothless Orange Man. "Who are those fellas parked outside? And who the feck are you?"

Quick as a shot, Wish-Wash turned to Toothless Orange Man. "I'm guessing Charlie forgot to tell you about Moose's Irish twin?" Then he addressed Joffa. "Lucky you came along. This bloke is from *Mission Impossible*. I think he was getting ready to explode."

Toothless Orange Man retreated outside.

They heard a car door slam, and watched the convoy drive away hastily.

Joffa's, Oodles's and Wish-Wash's eyes turned to Awesome Sauce, who threw his hands in the air.

"Technical hitch, OK? It wasn't supposed to play *Jangle Bells*. It was supposed to play AC/DC's *Hell's Bells*."

————

Joffa agreed to stay put at the museum while Oodles and Wish-Wash went to see Sergeant Stretch.

"I tink Tim and I need to talk, anyway," he said.

"Don't leave his side in case those heavies come back." Oodles said. "I don't want to return to find the building gone."

"You don't mind staying overnight too?" Wish-Wash asked.

"Let me guess?" Joffa said. "You'll set up the stretcher bed in the lounge room again?"

"It'll only be till Moose comes home."

"I tink that stretcher was designed for a jockey with fold-up legs. Why can't I sleep in Moose's bed if he isn't using it?"

"Don't be ridiculous," Wish-Wash said. "You know how he feels about other people sleeping in his bed?"

———

They found Stretch packing his fly-fishing gear and camping gear into the back of his SUV in the driveway of the new police station.

The policeman slapped his right knee when he heard footsteps and turned around. "I knew it couldn't be true. I don't know what *The Pick of the Crop* is playing at, but I'm sure glad neither of you is dead."

He had known them for a long time. They had both been very welcoming when he had arrived in the town as a young junior constable; in the early days, he had even boarded with Oodles and Madge.

"Got a minute?" Oodles said.

Stretch picked up on his frown. "Something wrong?"

"Very wrong," Wish-Wash said. "Perhaps we can tell you all we know over a cuppa? We don't know who might be eavesdropping."

Stretch scanned the empty street slowly, but didn't say he had spotted any snoopers. "You were lucky to catch me. I heard the trout are biting up on Bing Bong Mountain."

He led them down a path, into the police station portion of the building. "I had to come back inside anyway to change out of my uniform." He ushered them into his office. "Take a seat. I'll get that tea?"

Wish-Wash nodded. "And bickies if you have them."

Stretch left them in the room alone.

Other than a foolscap notepad opened at a fresh page and a silver-coloured pen beside it, the most prominent thing on the shiny desktop was their reflection. Stretch's blue hat hung on a stand in the corner of the room next to the filing cabinet. And a clock ticked loudly on the wall.

Some minutes later, Stretch returned with a tray and laid it down. "Sorry about the mismatched crockery. It's all I could find that was washed up."

"No worries," Oodles said. "I'm happy to take the cup." He looked around the room. "I do like your new digs."

"I forgot. This is your first time in here." Stretch pointed out the high ceiling. "You have to marvel at the workmanship of the convicts who built this place. If you look closely, some of the sandstone bricks bear their thumbprints."

"So it was a jail back in the early days of the town?"

"No, it was actually a bakery. Ironic, really. I wonder how many of the convict builders were sent to Van Diemen's Land for seven years for stealing a loaf of bread?"

Stretch started pouring from the blue-and-white porcelain teapot. "So? How can I help you blokes?"

Wish-Wash wrapped his hands around his mug, lifted it to his lips and blew on it. "Some lousy bludgers have just tried to demolish the museum. A fleet of trucks turned up outside and a thug in a hard-hat tried to tell us he had instructions to pull down the building and reassemble it in Slutz Plains."

Stretch lurched towards his hat. "Are they still there?"

"Sit down! Don't waste your time," Oodles said. "Joffa scared them away, and he's guarding the place in case they come back."

Stretch slumped back down in his chair on the other side of the desk. "Where did they reckon this order came from?"

Wish-Wash sprayed spittle and biscuit crumbs as his voice rose. "The head bloke showed me a forged document with my own flamin' signature supposedly on it. You believe that?"

"Do you have any idea who's behind it?"

Oodles and Wish-Wash shrugged in unison.

"Some weird stuff is going on in this town," Oodles said. "We think James Northan has been kidnapped."

Stretch nearly choked on a mouthful of tea. "Kidnapped?"

Wish-Wash added: "We like Messerschmitt for it. If you search his house, I'm sure you'll find Jimbo tied up."

Stretch stiffened. "We just can't rummage through a bloke's house looking for evidence that may or may not be there. That would be violating his rights."

"You know his German shepherd desecrates Colonel Northan's statue every day, don't you?" Oodles said.

"Adolf?"

Oodles held his gaze. "Who's Adolf?"

"That's what Messerschmitt calls his dog. I assumed you knew?"

Oodles clipped his empty cup and saucer as he stood up abruptly, making a clattering sound. "Adolf! That's got to be a crime, for starters. That blinking dog does number two's on the base of the statue every day."

"Does he?" Stretch's eyes popped. "How come no one's ever lodged a complaint?"

"Isn't it obvious?" Oodles said. "Messerschmitt has got everyone scared. And why wouldn't they be? If naming a dog Adolf isn't intimidatory, I don't know what is."

"Far as I know, no law prohibits people from naming their dogs anything they want."

"But Adolf? Doesn't that go against the Geneva Conventions?"

Stretch shrugged. "You named your dog Gough to get up James Northan's nose, didn't you?" After Gough Whitlam?

"You can't prove that?"

"It's common knowledge."

"So is the fact you also let Gough pee on the statue." This came from Wish-Wash, causing Oodles and Stretch to look at him.

Oodles spluttered: "Prove it!"

Stretch examined Oodles's face. "You do know that would be breaking the law?"

"I plead the fifth. Or is it the second?"

"This isn't America, Oodles," Stretch said sternly. "If I see such a thing, I'm going to have to issue you with a summons." He drummed his fingers on the desk. "So why do you think Messerschmitt is also behind the attempt to dismantle the museum?"

"We're going to have to bow to your investigative expertise on that one," Oodles croaked. "But Wish-Wash is pretty sure he stole all the missing signs because he's assembling a ransom note." He turned to Wish-Wash. "Aren't you?"

Wish-Wash nodded. "He also nicked the bench."

Stretch frowned. "The bench? What bench?"

"Surely someone told you?"

Stretch shook his head slowly.

Oodles flicked his head back and sighed. "My fault. You weren't here when I came to report it on Wednesday, and I've been distracted ever since. But, Gawd, we told Norm Hit about it so why there's been nothing in *The Pick of the Crop* is a mystery to me. I remember a time if anything had happened to that bench, it'd be front-page news. But not any more. The council gave up on the Colonel Richard Northan bench years ago. Since I *didn't* tell you, and Wish-Wash *didn't* tell you and James *couldn't* tell you, I guess I ought not be surprised *no one* told you."

Stretch picked up his pen, and sucked in a breath. "So when did this happen?"

Oodles shrugged. "Early Wednesday morning is our best guess. But the plot thickens. Wish-Wash and I saw the same bench reconstructed in Slutz Plains on Thursday."

Stretch stopped his writing and looked up. "You sure?"

"Of course I'm sure," Oodles said. "You know how many years I had to care for that bench?"

"And how many years he vandalised it?" Wish-Wash's comment attracted more glares. "What? What did I say?"

"It's our bench, all right," Oodles said. "They've filled in the holes with putty, and painted it red, but there is no doubt in my mind." He swallowed to get rid of an imagined bad taste in his mouth. "We went to see the mayor of Slutz Plains to demand an answer, but Manky Manning reckoned that bench is the same bench that's always been there. Why would he say that?"

Stretch stared into space. "I thought we had a real puzzle on our hands when the sign outside the rose garden turned up outside the sewerage plant, but these events are starting to take on Rubik's Cube proportions." He closed his eyes and scratched his head. "I need to think this through. Until some positive evidence comes to hand, I suggest everyone needs to calm down. I'll give it some more thought while I'm up the mountain."

"You're going fly-fishing at a time like this?" Oodles said.

"I thought you of all people would understand, Oodles? It'll give me some clear air to think this through. But don't worry. I'll be in radio contact with my constables."

Oodles exhaled loudly. "So, how did you know we weren't killed in that fireball anyway?"

"Easy. When I read the officer quoted was a Sergeant Schultz, I realised someone had been playing a joke on the newspaper." He looked from Oodles to Wish-Wash for a sign of recognition. "Sergeant Schultz? *Hogan's Heroes?* 'I know nussink?'"

"Oh, him?" Wish-Wash said.

"Then I thought about the consequences of such an accident. If a fiery accident occurred almost outside my front door, *I'd* know about it."

Oodles shook his head slowly. "I just can't work out why someone wants us pretend-dead? If they wait a few more years, they can have the real thing."

"Don't talk like that!" Stretch said. "You two are fixtures in this town. You'll be walking around long after I get my pension. Besides, I hear you're both off on an overseas trip soon so you must both be hale and healthy."

"Well, I am." Oodles smiled. "Doc Jenkins says I'm as fit as a Mallee bull."

"A very *old* Mallee bull," Wish-Wash said.

"I'm also the only one who's actually got a passport."

Wish-Wash glared at him. "You know as well as I do, Oodles, I've lodged my application and Katy reckons it'll be back on time."

"You *hope* it is. If it isn't, don't be surprised if I go on my own."

"On your own?" Wish-Wash looked at Stretch across the table. "You know he wanted to take me as his carer, only I told him he's big enough and ugly enough to carry his own bags?"

"Come off the grass." Oodles turned to Stretch. "You'll have to forgive Wish-Wash for his forgetfulness. The poor old fellow has just found out he's a grandfather."

———

"Why did you have to go and tell him that?" Wish-Wash said as the old men walked back down the High Street.

"It's the truth, isn't it?"

Wish-Wash blew out his cheeks. "Why are we walking back towards the museum, anyway? Shouldn't we be crossing the road so we can think this through over a cuppa at the cafe?"

Oodles stopped and turned, bringing Wish-Wash to a halt on the footpath. "You must have a cast-iron bladder! You've just *had* a blinking cuppa."

"Can I help it if I do my best thinking when I'm dunking biscuits?"

"I don't think we need any gastronomic help to work out what we need to do next. I think we're going to have to pay another visit to *The Pick of the Crop*."

Wish-Wash looked behind him bewilderedly. "Aren't we walking the wrong way?"

"Norm wouldn't be there this early in the day. He starts late on Saturdays on account of all the sporting results he has to write up. Bowls, cricket and the like."

"Great! So we have to walk there in the dark?"

"After the whingeing you did last time? No, I'll be outside the museum with my car at 5pm."

Wish-Wash's eyes widened. "Are you kidding? Last time you drove me, you got us both killed!"

Oodles set off down the footpath again. "Don't even joke about that, old cock. Just be grateful they'll let anyone into those newspaper offices, even men like you wearing yellow shirts with pink ties."

"I still don't know why you even need to come back to the museum?"

"Strewth! I can't leave Gough tied up outside the museum all day. Visitors will think *he* is the Tasmanian Tiger."

Norm didn't look as pleased to see them as Sergeant Stretch had.

"What now?" he said when he looked up from his computer.

Wish-Wash snarled at him. "We thought you'd want to hear the latest development. It made Sergeant Stretch very worried."

Norm looked up towards the framework of wooden beams supporting the tin roof. "It never rains but it pours." He stood up. "Out with it then. I really haven't got all day."

"A crew from a demolition firm turned up at the museum this morning," Wish-Wash said.

Norm squinted at him. "So . . . ?"

"So, they had falsified documents instructing them to pull the place down and reassemble it in Slutz Plains."

Norm looked roofwards again. It was hard to tell from his expression whether he was looking for God or for a rat scurrying along the rafters. "That's all I need. You know they've found the town boundary signs?"

"No! Where are they?" This came from Oodles who had sat down on a plastic chair on its own in the middle of the cavernous room. It didn't look like it was for visitors, and it wasn't Norm's chair.

Before Norm could reply, Wish-Wash said, "Let me guess? On the tip? With letters missing!"

Norm shook his head. "Nope, fully intact, I'm told. They weren't found at the tip either. But now we have a new theft. Someone has nicked the Slutz Plains boundary signs and replaced them with ours. I've just got off the phone with Mayor Manning, and he's furious."

"Good!" Wish-Wash scratched his chin. "Now he knows how we feel about the bench. You did ask him about that, didn't you?"

"It didn't seem like the time."

"You didn't think there might be a connection?" Oodles said. "First our bench winds up at Slutz Plains, then our town boundary signs go the same way."

"It's not my job to solve crimes, just to report on them. I leave the police work to Sergeant Stretch and his officers."

"You know Sergeant Shultz is not even a real person," Oodles said.

Norm glared at Oodles. "Don't think you can go on sitting on that chair for much longer. Barely Legal Leigh will be here soon to write his wine column."

Wish-Wash gasped. "What would he know about fine wine? His tastebuds have only ever experienced cheap plonk."

"That doesn't matter to my bosses," Norm said. "The only thing that matters to them is he's agreed to write the column for nothing just to get the experience. Head office said I'm to make sure a chair is available for him."

"You know he's planning to vacate the job of town drunk soon?" Wish-Wash said.

"Why would he?" Norm said. "He's only just got it!"

"Well. Don't say I didn't warn you!" Wish-Wash said.

Oodles looked around. "Shame there is not a computer for him."

Norm puffed out his cheeks. "That's why I was trying to get my work done before he comes in, so I can let him use mine while I take a break."

"Any news on James?"

Norm shook his head. "Only that Maddie is coming home tonight. She rang me last night. She doesn't know where her father is either. The good news is she'll know where the key is to his cottage."

As they were talking, the front door opened.

Oodles looked around and saw it was the wispy-faced Barely Legal Leigh, who was clearly horrified when he saw who else was in the room.

When Wish-Wash turned, they greeted each other like two snarling dogs.

———

Sunday morning

Oodles and Wish-Wash rang the bell at the Northan mansion. It must have been the servants' day off because Maddie opened the door.

Oodles nodded his greetings. "G'day, Madam Mayor. Sorry we meet under these circumstances."

Before she could answer, Norm emerged from the shadows behind her in the hallway. "I've got a bone to pick with you." He waved a finger at Wish-Wash, who had come dressed in his fake cow-skin trousers with the black-and-white blotches.

"I don't know what you said to Barely Legal Leigh as you were leaving," Norm said, "but whatever it was it propelled him into one of the worst cases of writer's block I've ever seen. Do you know how many hours it took him to write 350 words? I didn't get home till after midnight."

"At least you *did* get home," Wish-Wash said. "Poor Jimbo hasn't been home for days."

Maddie sighed. "I wouldn't worry," she said with a voice honed by the best girls' private school in the country. "Do you not remember how Daddy disappeared without telling us four or five years ago?"

"Yes, but this is different," Oodles said. "I don't think he has the money nowadays to fly to Alice Springs for a week."

"Hmm, yes, you're right. Thanks to you." As she said it, she gave him a piercing look. "But it is quite possible he has gone to a writer's retreat somewhere close. Did Norm not tell you? Daddy's writing poetry."

"But what if he isn't? What if something has happened to him?"

"Like what?"

"We're pretty sure we can rule out suicide," Wish-Wash chirped. "I mean an uppity bloke like Jimbo wouldn't have to top himself. He'd have lots of people lined up to help him."

Maddie's lips quivered.

"So, we reckon he's probably been kidnapped," Wish-Wash said.

An exasperated voice came from behind Maddie. "Didn't I warn you they'd say that, dear?"

"We reckon Messerschmitt's got him," Wish-Wash said. "I'm surprised you let reprobates like him live in this town!"

"I have no idea who you might be talking about," Maddie said.

"No? You'll probably receive a wooden ransom note from him very soon," Wish-Wash said.

"A ransom note?"

"Yes, we'll also need to check out his granny flat. Oodles saw a note through the kitchen window."

"Oh, that?" Maddie flashed her politician's smile. "Yes, I found that when I checked his house earlier."

"What does it say?" Oodles said.

"If you must know it says *three potatoes, a bag of green beans, six red apples and a T-bone steak.*"

Oodles threw his hands to his temples. "It was a shopping list?"

"Unless it is cryptic code from the kidnappers?" Maddie faux-laughed.

"So there is no need for me and Wish-Wash to look through his house then?" Oodles said.

"It would be a complete waste of time," Maddie said. "Besides, I'm not sure Daddy would appreciate you two going through his things. Especially the cow."

———

They decided an early morning-tea was in order.

The Wind Tunnel Cafe had began opening on Sunday mornings in the hope of tempting people on the way home from church who possibly wanted to get rid of the taste of cheap communion wine.

"You're in early." Wendy looked up when they came through the bead curtains.

"You're lucky to get *any* customers with those curtains," Wish-Wash said, dragging a chair out. "I couldn't be the only one who finds them annoying."

"They keep out the blow-flies," Wendy said. "Except for you. Who's minding the museum?"

"Joffa and Awesome Sauce are on duty until Moose comes home from hospital," Oodles said.

"Moose has promised to tear Awesome Sauce a new one if he even dares to tinker with my door chimes again," Wish-Wash fumed.

"Don't mind grumpy bum." Oodles took a seat opposite Wish-Wash. "He ought to be more worried about men coming in wearing hard-hats than being subjected to a few bars of inappropriate music. I'd just feel comfortable knowing Moose is glaring at the demolition men, rather than Awesome Sauce trying to stare them down."

Wish-Wash grumbled. "I think I need extra biscuits today."

"We've just been to see Maddie Northan." Oodles sighed. "I remember when she used to be a nice little girl."

"Oh her?" Wendy wiped the table with her cloth. "I've only met her once. She was in full campaign mode at the school fair. The apple doesn't fall far from the tree, does it?"

"You're not wrong," Oodles said.

"She called me a cow," Wish-Wash said, "which is like the pot calling the kettle black."

Wendy stood back and eyed the tabletop. "You told her about your concerns about Messerschmitt?"

"She didn't seem to care," Oodles said.

"You know Messerschmitt's dog is named Adolf," Wish-Wash said.

"Is it? Well, I never . . ." Wendy stared out the window towards the statue, which hadn't yet had its daily bombing.

Oodles looked out the window too. "Pity the latest in the Northan line doesn't have a statue in her likeness."

"What are we going to do about Jimbo?" Wish-Wash said.

"What can we do?" Oodles dropped his head. "Stretch doesn't want to look, Norm doesn't think it's his job, and Maddie doesn't think it's even a problem he's missing."

Wish-Wash raised a finger. "Hmm, I have an idea."

EIGHT
SPIES LIKE US

THE OLD MEN were kneeling on opposite sides of the stretcher bed in the lounge upstairs at the museum.

They were trying to make sense of the crackling radio handset lying between them.

It was nearly 5pm, and Joffa was downstairs behind the reception desk.

Wish-Wash and Oodles had begged him to stay longer in case those hard-hatted men came back.

"My back is killing me," Joffa had said. "Besides, Katy *will* kill me if I stay out again!"

"I'll talk to Katy," Oodles had said. "It's only till Moose comes home."

Wish-Wash adjusted his suspenders as he knelt by the stretcher. He was still wearing his blotchy black-and-white trousers but he had changed into a light-green shirt and a dark-green tie that almost blended with his camo trousers, especially if you were going for the upside-down Holstein cow-in-the-meadow look.

Oodles and Wish-Wash leaned in on either side of the stretcher, but all the radio was emitting was white noise.

"Is this thing even working?" Wish-Wash picked it up and spoke into the microphone. "Rubber ducky, rubber ducky, ten-four, come in good buddy."

"What are you doing?" Oodles scowled at him, as the stretcher creaked beneath his weight. "You'll have every truckie within cooee talking back."

Awesome Sauce's voice came crackling back.

"Where are you, Spinner?" Wish-Wash said. "Over."

"I'm on the corner of Hill Street, like you said. I have a clear line of sight to the target's house. Over."

"Any sign of the target yet? Over."

"Nothing. Over."

"Be careful out there. Over and out." Wish-Wash put the radio handset back on the bed.

"*Be careful out there*?" Oodles croaked. "Really?"

"We have a duty of care to that kid, no matter what we think of him. Though I have to say Awesome Sauce is stretching my patience again. Didn't I say he wasn't to mention actual street names on the air?"

He wasn't wrong. Wish-Wash had stipulated this very firmly in the cafe.

It had taken three pots of tea, 26 digestives and two hours to map out The Mission.

Awesome Sauce was only to be referred to as Spinner, and was supposed to talk only in code, lest someone was electronically eavesdropping and could fathom out what was going on. Messerschmitt's abode was to be referred to only as Stalag 79. Hill Street was to be called Hilslwasse Strasse. Messerschmitt was to be referred to as *the target*.

The hope was the target would leave Stalag 79 unguarded long enough for the old men to break in and rescue James.

Oodles hadn't thought it was such a good idea to even send Awesome Sauce. But Wish-Wash had insisted.

Wendy had gone back to the kitchen and no one else was in the room, so Wish-Wash hadn't even needed to whisper. But he did, just as he made a point of constantly stirring sugar into his cup to muffle conversation.

"The walls could have flamin' ears."

"They'd want to be better than mine," Oodles said, "because I'm finding it hard to hear a word you say."

But what he did hear actually made sense. Oodles and Wish-Wash could hardly go on surveillance. Messerschmitt would spot them a mile off in his street. At his size, Joffa would stand out even more.

Awesome Sauce would be a new face to Messerschmitt. He'd be able to blend in.

The radio crackled back into life. "The target is leaving Stalag 79. Over. I repeat: he's on the move. Over."

Wish-Wash rubbed his hands together. "I love it when a plan comes together." He paused. "I only hope Messerschmitt's men aren't intercepting this though."

"Messerschmitt's men?" Oodles said. "What? You reckon he's raised an army of mercenaries, do you?"

Wish-Wash scowled. "You should feel privileged I'm even letting you listen in on this top-secret mission. Would you feel better waiting outside?"

Oodles ignored this. "Now what? Can we tell Spinner to return to base?" As soon as he said it, he knew why Wish-Wash had chosen that codename. Come in, spinner. Gawd!

Wish-Wash smiled.

"No, not yet." He spoke into the transmitter. "Good work, but stay at your post, Spinner. We don't want the target to think you're following him to the pub. Over."

Oodles rolled his eyes.

"Why did you even have to go and mention the pub on-air?" he croaked.

"I didn't say which pub, did I?"

"You muppet! Windy Mountain has only got one pub."

Wish-Wash smacked his forehead, and got back on the radio. "I repeat. Do not follow target back to the *Apple Strudel*. Over."

"Oh, good one!" Oodles said. "Awesome Sauce will have no idea what you're talking about now!"

"Smarty pants kid like that? He'll work it out."

"What makes you think Messerschmitt is headed for the pub anyway? Isn't it closed today?"

Wish-Wash tapped his nose. "That intel is top secret." He sighed noisily. "I suppose you need to know though. Don't you remember Rog serves select customers behind closed doors on Sundays?"

"Is he still doing that?"

"You don't think Rog shut up shop just because you don't go any more?"

———

Wish-Wash and Oodles went outside to stand on the footpath and wait for Messerschmitt to arrive.

Wish-Wash lit up a smoke just as Messerschmitt came swaggering towards them carrying a jerry can.

"Funny thing to be taking to the pub," Oodles said.

"I dunno," Wish-Wash said. "Maybe some two-stroke fuel fell off the back of a truck and he's offering it cheap to his mates. That kind of thing goes on in places like that."

Oodles nodded because he knew it was true.

But why Wish-Wash had to wave to Messerschmitt and say through a haze of smoke "How y'going?" was another one of life's little mysteries.

———

They watched him disappear down the side path, which led to the back bar.

Wish-Wash stubbed out his half-smoked cigarette with his foot, then reached inside his trouser pocket and pulled out a black, woollen balaclava.

"You must be joking," Oodles said.

"I don't want to be seen."

"You reckon that will work, do you? It's stinking hot, and it's still broad daylight. You'll stick out like a sore thumb."

"But no one will know it's me," Wish-Wash said.

"Really? How many oversized pin cushions wear such loud shirts and such questionable trousers in this town? Where do you even go to buy those strides anyway? A dairy?"

Wish-Wash looked wounded. "You're the second person to criticise my trousers." He looked down. "What exactly is wrong with them?"

"Nothing. I don't know why the Army hasn't adopted that camo pattern?"

Wish-Wash stuffed the balaclava back in his pocket. "C'mon, let's get this done." He charged off down the street, Oodles struggling to keep up.

"What's the big hurry? Messerschmitt will likely be in the pub until closing time."

Wish-Wash stopped and turned. "Jimbo might be running out of air."

Oodles looked at him, puzzled.

"You're the one who said he must be gagged."

"That doesn't mean he can't breathe through his nose."

Wish-Wash started walking with a purpose again.

"Wait up, will you?" Oodles started after him. "I don't get it. You've always detested James, now you want to save him."

Wish-Wash stopped abruptly and turned around with hands on hips.

"For your information, I hate Messerschmitt even more."

"Gawdsake! You just said hello to him! You were fine with him sitting on *our* bench! Now you hate him! What's all that about?"

Wish-Wash grunted. "You've never heard of not revealing your hand? Staying poker faced? Deep down, I was furious. I hoped if he sat on the bench often enough, it would collapse beneath him."

"*We* sit there!"

"Yes, but I always make sure you and I are at the ends so we have something to hang on to when it comes crashing in."

"What about when James used to join us?"

"Why do you think I always made him sit in the middle?"

Oodles shook his head. "You didn't think that through, did you? Guess who would have had to pull the splinters out of James's backside?"

Wish-Wash stomped the pavement with one of his cow legs. "It hardly matters now the bench isn't across the road any more. What matters is I have a score to settle with Messerschmitt."

"Why are you suddenly so worked up?"

"Do you really want to know?" Wish-Wash stamped the concrete with his other hoof. "My intel is he's been sitting on *my* stool every night."

"Which stool?"

"The one that's got a plate with my name engraved on it. *For stellar services to the town as town drunk.*"

"Is that stool still there?"

Wish-Wash puffed out his cheeks. "They moved it to the back bar."

"What's it matter, anyway? That was a part of your life you left behind years ago."

"Can't a bloke still be proud of his achievements? You don't under-stand, do you? I sat on that stool for 13 years. Even though I was forced to leave, the stool stayed, and it was passed like a trophy from one town drunk to the next — until that namby-pamby Barely Legal Leigh gave it up to Messerschmitt."

Now Oodles witnessed something he had never seen happen before. Wish-Wash spat on the road. "And don't give me that nonsense that Messerschmitt is next in line for the job. Nothing happens until it happens. With any luck, him and bloody Adolf will be lingering around the statue next time you run into it."

"Will you listen to yourself?" Oodles shouted. *"That never happened!"*

When they climbed the hill to Hilslwasse Strasse, they saw Awesome Sauce straighten up from the lamp-post he had been leaning on.

"I was awaiting further instructions, sir." He held up his radio handset as they came into earshot.

"We thought it best to deliver the message in person." Wish-Wash used a hand to survey Messerschmitt's tiny fibro cottage against the sinking sun. "What can you tell me, son?"

"It's not going to be easy, sir."

"Sir? Son?" Oodles said.

Wish-Wash looked daggers at him. "Not everyone is failing to take this operation seriously."

"A vicious-looking dog is patrolling the perimeter, sir." Awesome Sauce clicked his heels together.

Oodles pointed from Awesome Sauce to Wish-Wash. "When did you decree he had to call you sir?"

Wish-Wash snorted. "That's the problem with you, Oodles. You don't understand the importance of the chain of command." He turned back to Awesome Sauce. "The dog's a German shepherd, am I correct, son?"

"How did you know that, sir?"

Wish-Wash tapped the side of his nose. "Intel. Need-to-know basis."

"I guess you already know it's a brute of a dog, sir?"

"I do, son. I do. The problem is: how do we get past the mutt long enough to get a look through the windows." He turned to Oodles. "Any ideas?"

Oodles shrugged, but then he pointed to a figure coming up the hill. "You could ask him, General?"

Wish-Wash's eyes nearly popped out when he saw it was Messer-schmitt. "Christ. Just try to act normally, men."

Fat chance of that, thought Oodles. What was the likelihood of a gangly kid holding a radio handset with a protruding aerial, a man wearing cow-camo trousers whose pocket bore the bulge of a thick woollen balaclava and an 85-year-old man without his customary dog appearing normal?

But Messerschmitt didn't even appear to notice, probably because his face was blackened.

"I can't believe it." Messerschmitt shook his head as he walked past. "There is only one pub in town, and now it's burning down."

————

It was like following a one-cow stampede. Oodles and Awesome Sauce struggled to keep up with Wish-Wash as he ran down the hill.

Now they were wrestling at the side of one of the firetrucks parked out front of The Applecart as smoke billowed from cracked windows and from underneath the edges of the roof.

Men in yellow protective jackets were coming in and out of the pub, stepping over the water pipes snaking from the trucks.

Lucky Joffa was also there. He helped them stop Wish-Wash from running into the smouldering building.

"There is nothing you can do," Oodles said. "Doggie and his men are doing their best to save it."

The grey-haired Doggie Dougall stepped out of the smoke. "Oodles is right, Wish-Wash. We're doing everything we can."

"Why aren't you inside, then?" Wish-Wash screamed. "Shouldn't every man be at the pump?"

Doggie swept a yellow arm towards the pub. "I'd just be getting in the way." He nodded down to the radio transmitter in his hands. "My men are giving me regular reports."

Wish-Wash and Doggie hadn't been friends for a long time. In fact, they barely talked to each other. Doggie used to be the town's dogcatcher, but the powers-that-be had decided there wasn't enough work to keep him busy in that job so they had made him the town fire chief.

He was in charge of five firefighters and two fire trucks, which were housed just two doors up, on the other side of the pub.

Mostly he just sat in his office while his men tinkered with the engines.

But Oodles guessed he was here today so he could finally fly the flag, and help convince taxpayers they were getting value for money.

"Anyone dead?" Oodles said.

Doggie shook his head. "If this had happened this time last night the place would be teeming with people. But Rog and Messerschmitt were the only ones inside, and they got out before the fire really got going."

His radio crackled into life and he spoke into it. "Old Fart, receiving, over." He looked up and smiled. "It's a little in-joke between the men and me."

"We've located the hotel register, Old Fart. Someone by the name of Tim Noah the Fourth is registered as staying here. We're looking for his corpse now. Over."

Doggie gave Oodles a pained look. "I take that back about no one being dead. It'd be just my luck to lose a visiting monarch."

Oodles burst into a smile.

"I don't see what's funny?" Doggie said. "This is my first actual fire, and I had been hoping to come through it with a zero fatality rate."

Oodles looked from Awesome Sauces's face to Doggie's. "Doggie, meet Tim Noah the Fourth."

Doggie did something between a bow and a curtsy. "So glad you're OK, Your Holiness."

"He's not a fecking king nor a fecking pope," Joffa said. "He's my new fecking partner."

Only now did Oodles realise Joffa was meant to be minding the museum. "What are you doing here? What if this is a diversion, so the men in the hard-hats can sneak back and start dismantling the museum?"

"Relax the cacks," Joffa said. "Moose has come back from hospital and propped himself up behind the counter. I came out to see if I could help." He shook his head. "When I got out here, Rog was sitting on the kerb, coughing, with his head in his hands but Messerschmitt was halfway up the High Street."

The Wish-Wash volcano erupted again. "Why didn't you make a citizen's arrest? I bet Messerschmitt still had a box of matches in his hand!"

Joffa's eyes widened. "You tink he did this?"

"I know he did it. Oodles and me saw him take a jerry can into the pub." He turned around to Oodles. "Didn't we, cobber?"

"To be fair to him, it might have been empty."

"The can didn't look empty to me the way he was carrying it!" Wish-Wash pointed to the building. "That's part of my golden past going up in smoke."

Wish-Wash turned towards Joffa. "Was Rog carrying anything out when he escaped?"

"Not that I saw," Joffa said. "Like what?"

"Only the flamin' honour board and my old stool! If Barely Legal Leigh had been doing his job properly he would have been at the pub to prevent Messerschmitt from burning the place down. Ahhh."

Joffa was too quick for him. He grabbed Wish-Wash by the suspenders as soon as the old man broke away towards the fire again. Wish-Wash bounced back like someone doing a bungee jump and Joffa caught him as he flew backwards.

Oodles waved a finger at the stunned Wish-Wash, as he stumbled to regain his balance. "Now why did you have to do that?"

"We've just about got it under control," Doggie said.

"Like I'm going to trust you with the truth, Doggie." The corners of Wish-Wash's mouth were flecked with white foam. "It's not your stool in jeopardy."

He broke free of Joffa. "Damn Messerschmitt. Even if it wasn't him who lit the match, which is *very* unlikely, if he had had any respect for history, he would have put his life on the line to save that stool."

"I'm sure it'll be all right." Oodles looked to Doggie.

But Doggie shook his head. "Old timber building like this! The only reason it's still standing is we got here quickly, but I'd guess the structural damage is substantial."

Oodles tried to draw something positive out of him. "But things can be salvaged, right?"

Doggie shook his head again. "I doubt it. One blackened stool will look like the next blackened stool."

"But what about the honour boards?" Oodles said.

Doggie shrugged. "Depends which wall they were hanging on. My men report two walls have collapsed."

Doggie's transmitter crackled into life again.

But this time it was a pizza delivery driver, who could not find where he had to go to deliver one Hawaiian deep crust, a piece of garlic bread and a soft drink.

"I wish those people would get off our frequency!" Doggy said. "Would you believe we had some Germans clogging up the airwaves earlier?"

———

Moose pinched his nostrils shut when Joffa, Awesome Sauce, Wish-Wash and Oodles came in the door. "You blokes smell like you've been rolling in the ashes."

Wish-Wash glared at him. "Don't even joke about that?"

Moose bowed his head. "Sorry, Wish-Wash. I know how much that pub meant to you."

"Do you?" Wish-Wash said. "Do you really!" He turned around and looked from eye to eye. "Why did you rotten wasters hold me back?"

Wish-Wash slumped into one of the chairs in the reception area and put his head into his hands. "What am I going to do now? I spent my glory years in that pub!"

Moose broke into a smile. "I know you'll find this hard to believe, Wish-Wash, but this is actually your lucky day. An email came in for you while you were out."

Wish-Wash looked up. "You've been reading my flamin' emails?"

"It was hard not to the way this computer is set up. It comes up in the preview panel."

"I can assure you it doesn't," Wish-Wash said.

Awesome Sauce coughed nervously. "Didn't I tell you I had changed the way it presents? I thought you'd like it that way."

Wish-Wash glanced over to Oodles, who had settled on another chair. They both rolled their eyes.

Wish-Wash sighed wearily. "OK, the damage is done. Read it to me, big fella."

"Is that wise?" Oodles said. "It might be a love letter from your internet bride."

"Oh, very funny," Wish-Wash said. "Go on, read it, Moose. Anything will brighten the day I'm having."

Moose fumbled around on the keyboard to bring up the email. "Are you ready for this?" He did a little drum roll on the side of the plastic keyboard.

"Come on, out with it," Wish-Wash said.

Moose tapped the screen with a finger. "It says here you've inherited a castle."

Wish-Wash leapt to his feet and headed towards the reception bench. "What are you on about?" He lifted the gate in the counter and went to stand behind Moose.

Oodles could see his lips moving as he silently read the email. He stared into space.

"Well?" Joffa said. "What does it say?"

"You're not going to like it, my Irish friend," Moose said. "The email shows a picture of the castle Wish-Wash has inherited in County Donegal, and my guess is it's bigger than the one you have in Dublin."

"That wouldn't be hard. Ours was a council flat, and we never owned it anyway."

Oodles stood up and headed towards the counter.

"It looks ridgy-didge," Wish-Wash said. "The email says it's from one of my distant relatives, Malachy Willson, who traced me through that DNA connection."

Oodles lifted the gate and came closer to see.

"Wow," Oodles said as he studied the pictures of the castle on the screen, which showed an impressive tower overlooking the sea. "We'll be able to have our own sleeping wings."

NINE
ROOM AT THE TOP
MONDAY MORNING AGAIN

WISH-WASH WAS STANDING on the footpath in front of the burnt-out pub when Oodles approached.

From a distance, he looked bright enough in his red shirt, yellow trousers and wearing a green tie. But when Oodles pulled up, the dark bags under his eyes told him that Wish-Wash hadn't slept well.

Wish-Wash's attention was on the workers carrying out blackened remains. Most of the rubble was thrown into the tray of Manny Hjorth's battered red truck, which had just returned from the tip.

"No sign of any of the stools?" Oodles asked.

Wish-Wash shook his head. "Truth is, I've given up on them bringing my stool out. I'm just on the look-out now for one piece of memorabilia I can pass on to my grandson."

Oodles studied his worried face. "So you've decided to accept him, then?"

"I didn't say that!" Wish-Wash cried. "I just want to leave my options open."

He examined Oodles, who was dressed in his old suit and had slicked back his hair with hair-cream. "You don't normally doll up to walk Gough, cobber?" He looked around and realised the dog was nowhere in sight.

"I'm on the way to mass," Oodles said.

Wish-Wash made an exaggerated sniffing sound. "Smelling like that?"

"For your information, Madge bought me this cologne. *You* smell like you dabbed au-de-smoke behind your ears."

Wish-Wash's eyes followed another man emerging from inside the pub carrying a blackened beer keg that he threw into the back of the truck. "Tell you what I did see come out? Remember the old jukebox?"

"I thought Rog had got rid of that years ago?" Oodles said.

"He must have just bunged it in a cupboard when it stopped working."

Wish-Wash squinted at another man who emerged carrying three blackened trophies.

Oodles suspected one of those trophies bore *his* name. He had been captain of The Applecart team that finished runner-up to Slutz Plains in the pub trivia regional finals in 2004. He might have been more cut up if they had won the blinking thing.

"Is Moose minding the shop?" Oodles got his answer immediately when he looked towards the museum and a figure on the other side of the glass waved at him.

Wish-Wash balled up a fist. "I've told him to not let Awesome Sauce anywhere near the computer."

"Where *is* the kid?" Oodles said.

Wish-Wash rolled his eyes. "Upstairs, worse luck. Since he's now homeless and Joffa's gone home, I let him sleep on the stretcher. I ought to have known no good would come of it."

"What did Moose sleep on?"

"He dragged some cushions on to the floor in the foyer. He said he'd feel more at home if he could build a campfire." Wish-Wash's face grew redder.

"Calm down! I'm sure he was only joking," Oodles said.

Wish-Wash pointed a shaking finger towards an upstairs window.

"I didn't think for one minute that the stretcher being near the book-case would be any kind of a problem. But Awesome Sauce has only taken it upon himself to rearrange all my sci-fi books by colour." He pointed to spots on an imaginary bookcase in the air. "Blue books here, yellow books there, red books bunched together."

Oodles tried not to laugh, but even though his mouth was shut, small wisps of air escaped his lips.

"Oh you think that's funny, do you? He's also indexed all my detective DVDs. By the year they came out!"

Wish-Wash squeezed his eyes shut. "I told him if he knows what's good for him, he's not to come back downstairs until he's put every book and DVD back in its proper order."

———

Oodles left Wish-Wash in his misery and continued towards the stone bridge over the lower reaches of the Bing Bong River, beyond which was the rebuilt Catholic Church.

It was where Father O'Boring and Billy Gumboots had died at the hands of arsonists.

The brick structure had sprung up from its own ashes in a matter of months, thanks to parishioners who had cleared the burnt-out rubble and provided free labour.

Mass on Sundays had resumed eight months ago. But Oodles just couldn't come at rejoining the two-faced flock who gathered outside the church after the service to exchange nasty gossip.

Today would have been manna from heaven for them.

Oodles could see the likely scene unfolding in his head as he walked. He'd let them sermonise how the pub had had it coming, how good had triumphed over alcoholic evil, and other sanctimonious diatribe. Then he'd drop into the conversation that he and Wish-Wash were going to Ireland. He could just about see the look of horror on Daisy Rowbottom's face. Then he'd twist the knife. *Yes, really. My travel partner is the same bloke who used to sleep in the bus shelter. At the business-class end of an A-380 yes. We're staying in Wish-Wash's castle in Donegal. Who knew he had such rich forebears?'*

Then reality set in.

It was Monday, which meant he'd only actually have an audience of one. There'd be no gossip, only more God stuff.

When Oodles had come clean about carving a notch in the park bench every time he went to mass on Sundays, Sergeant Stretch, Dr Jenkins and Father O'Flaherty had all invoked the name of God to solve the problem.

"The law has room for compassion," Stretch had said. "But for God's sake, don't do it again."

"God helps those who help themselves." Doc Jenkins handed him a prescription for anti-depressants. "You need to take these every day for the rest of your life. You hear?"

"Why don't you let me celebrate a private mass for you on Monday mornings?" Father O'Flaherty had said. "I'm sure Madge wouldn't want your ill-health on her conscience. I know God will be glad to see you any day of the week."

————

When Oodles returned home from church, he changed back into his overalls and set out to walk Gough.

They both had springs in their steps as they headed to the town centre.

It was only when Oodles looked up as they went to cross the High Street to the statue that his demeanour changed.

Messerschmitt was looking up at the towering bronze figure.

Oodles would have bet money the wild-haired man would be lying low after the fire at the pub. But, no, there he was, brazen as ever.

Oodles turned around to go back the way he came.

But it was too late. Messerschmitt growled. "Give us a hand, old man."

Oodles turned around again. "I was just, er, walking my dog."

"This'll only take a jiffy." Messerschmitt beckoned with a finger for him to cross.

Oodles shrugged, and pointed down to his dog.

"For fuck's sake," Messerschmitt said. "Just tie him to that post next to you. If I have to come over there I'll tie the rope around his scrawny little neck."

Next thing Oodles knew, he was holding one end of a retractable measuring tape Messerschmitt uncoiled from a shiny little dispenser.

"Stand here." Messerschmitt started walking around the statue, pulling out more tape as he went. He reappeared coming around the other side. "Now hold this end over the top of your end," he ordered.

Messerschmitt reached into a pocket and pulled out a notebook that he tucked under his chin. He plunged his hand into another pocket and produced a builder's pencil.

He pinned the notebook against the statue and wrote something down before relieving Oodles of his end of the measuring tape. The metal tape made a bouncy, swishing noise as it retracted with the push of a button.

Messerschmitt looked up again and scratched his head. "I'm guessing you're no good at climbing?"

Oodles was shaking, but managed to lie, "Anything higher than bathroom scales gives me vertigo."

Messerschmitt kept looking up. "How tall would you guess the structure is?"

Oodles feigned ignorance. "I can only measure things in tea bags. One for each person, and one for the pot."

Messerschmitt gave him a scorching look. "Are you shitting me, Oodles?"

Oodles knew exactly how tall it was. It had once been his job to know. The horrible thought crossed Oodles's mind that Messerschmitt was trying to work out how to get James's severed head up to the top! And Oodles certainly didn't want to be an accomplice to the grisly flaunting of James's decapitated head.

Oodles looked up again. It was then he realised Messerschmitt might have another grisly plan in mind.

But Messerschmitt interrupted his train of thought.

"How do you think this statue would look in the Main Street of Slutz Plains?"

————

Oodles did not to look back as he dragged Gough back along the High Street towards the museum.

Oodles didn't care about the dog's disappointment they had walked straight past the gate to the park. He needed to tell Wish-Wash what had happened.

As they neared the museum, he could see salvage work on the pub had finished for the day.

The front windows had been boarded up and tape saying THIS IS A POLICE INVESTIGATION SITE, DO NOT CROSS had been strung across the front of the block.

Oodles tied Gough to the lamp-post by the museum parking area, and went inside.

He didn't know what to expect from the door chimes, so he was relieved to hear nothing when he stepped inside.

When he looked up, he got an unexpected shock though. The counter had been wrapped in tape that declared it was also a POLICE INVESTIGATION SITE.

"Gawdsake! Don't tell me?" Oodles said as he approached Wish-Wash, who was sitting behind the desk. "You've been scammed? You don't really own a castle at all."

"Nothing of the sort," Wish-Wash said. "You're allowed to cross the line. It's Awesome Sauce I want to keep out."

Oodles leaned on the counter. "You nicked the police tape from next door, didn't you? You know they'll find out. You can't buy that stuff from Bunnings!"

"I only took the end bits flapping in the wind. The way I see it, I'm making taxpayers' money go further."

"I doubt Stretch will see it that way. This is likely to get him offside, just when I need to go see him again."

"What's so urgent?"

"I just helped Messerschmitt measure up the statue."

"What?" Wish-Wash squinted across the counter. "Why hasn't be been arrested yet? Why would he be measuring up the statue? And why would you be helping him?"

"I just happened to arrive as he was doing it, and he told me to hold the tape."

"Did he threaten you?"

"He named me by name again and he probably knows where I live."

"Did he say why he was interested in the measurement of the statue?"

Oodles stepped back and folded his arms. "I didn't dare ask but I have two theories. He might be checking to see if it'll take the weight of James's severed head."

Wish-Wash smiled. "I doubt that would weigh much."

"Please don't joke about that, old cock?"

"What's your other theory?"

"He's trying to work out how easy it would be to relocate the statue to Slutz Plains."

Wish-Wash frowned. "Why would he do that?"

"He gave them our bench, didn't he?"

"Yes, but the statue is different. Slutz Plains would have to nominate someone who looks like Colonel Northan."

"Whatever, I'm sure Stretch will want to know."

"Have you forgotten he's gone fishing up on Bing Bong Mountain? That's why he didn't attend the fire at the pub."

Oodles pinched the bridge of his nose. "He might be back now his crime tape has gone missing."

"How would he find out? A couple of his young constables were back next door this morning, but even they've scarpered now."

Oodles side-stepped towards the gate in the counter. He lifted the tape and ducked under it, then he lifted the gate. "So where is everyone?"

"Moose has gone for a hobble in the gallery to see if anything needs updating. Awesome Sauce is still upstairs righting what he put wrong."

"He still hasn't got the books back where they were?"

Wish-Wash shook his head rapidly. "I don't know how many times I've had to go upstairs." He counted out on his fingers. "No, I don't want them in order of the year of flamin' printing; no, I don't want them in order of flamin' publisher; he even put them in alphabetical order of titles, you believe that?"

———

The only trace of Sergeant Stretch's SUV was a small puddle of oil on the concrete driveway.

Oodles walked around the back of the building. Even though the blinds were closed, Oodles tried the door but the station was locked. A phone inside rang and rang but nobody answered it. He went around the front and knocked on the door to the residence Stretch shared with his wife Elaine. There wasn't a sound.

"C'mon Gough, let's go home," Oodles said to the little dog at his feet.

He had been ready to tell Stretch all three of his theories of what Messerschmitt might be planning.

He had spared Wish-Wash one of his hypotheses.

In his opinion, the top of that statue had room for at least three severed heads. James's, Wish-Wash's and his own noggin.

TEN

IT'S A LONG WAY TO THE TOP

DREAMTIME EARLY ON TUESDAY
MORNING

"NICE VIEW," James Northan's severed head said. "I wonder why we never thought about congregating up here before?"

Oodles would have shrugged if he had possessed a body. "We never needed this vista when we had the bench to sit on, old cock. We could see all the way up the High Street."

"But we couldn't see from this direction," Wish-Wash said. "And not from this elevated vantage point either."

Like the other old men, his head was speared on a rusty spike sticking up from Colonel Northan's hat. A cigarette bounced up and down in his mouth as he spoke and he probably wished he had hands so he could wave the smoke away.

Oodles woke up coughing.

He reached over and grabbed the clock from the bedside table and brought it closer so he could read the time.

4.45am! Gawdsake!

Oodles didn't dare try falling back to sleep in case he slipped back into his terrifying nightmare.

He climbed out of bed and dressed.

He opened the curtains, and then pulled up the wood-framed

window. The birds had already started their morning scales, and the smell of coming rain was in the air.

───────

Gough would normally be straining on his lead as soon as he heard anyone approach him. But he only poked his head out of his kennel as Oodles trudged across the lawn in the half-light.

The dog yawned as he got to his feet and took himself outside the doghouse.

Oodles clipped the lead on to his collar. "Let's go, mate, before the the heavens open."

No one stirred as they walked down the hill in the murk. Even the early risers in the town were still asleep. It was too early even for the municipal street cleaners with their blowers.

Normally the street lights would still be on this early in the day, but they weren't for some reason.

If Oodles hadn't had his head down scanning for doggy do-do on the High Street footpath, he might have noticed what was wrong earlier.

But he was outside the Wind Tunnel Cafe before he looked up and saw it. Or rather didn't see it. The statue of Colonel Northan was gone!

───────

"Wake up." Oodles shook Wish-Wash by the shoulder. "The statue has gone."

Wish-Wash opened his eyes, and jumped. "What the flamin' heck are you doing in my bedroom?"

"Moose let me in. Quick, we need to do something. Messerschmitt has nicked the statue."

Wish-Wash sat up. "Colonel Northan's statue?" He rubbed his eyes. "When?"

"Last night when we were sleeping."

"But how could one bloke just remove it? Wouldn't you need cranes and lots of workmen, floodlights, oxy-acetylene torches and a fleet of trucks?" Wish-Wash swung round to a sitting position on the edge of the bed and reached down to retrieve his trousers from the floor. Oodles looked up with the intention of averting his eyes, but he still got a good view.

"I thought you were going to get rid of that mirror above the bed," Oodles said.

"When have I had a flamin' chance? Anyway, it's not my bed."

"What are you talking about?"

Wish-Wash pointed to the empty single bed at the other end of the room as he crossed the room and opened a wardrobe. He turned around with one arm in an Hawaiian shirt. "I'm just keeping the big fella's king-size bed warm while he's stuck downstairs. You won't tell him, will you?"

The room smelt like an ashtray. Cigarette butts had been squashed out in an old saucer on the bedside table.

Wish-Wash buttoned up the shirt and selected a striped tie to go with it. "I'll ring Katy and Joffa. They must have heard something from their place."

"Didn't I tell you!" Oodles said. "Messerschmitt *was* measuring the statue up for the Slutz Plains Council. What I want to know is how Manky Manning thinks he will get away with this?"

———

Joffa and Katy weren't answering. "Where the flamin' heck are they?" Wish-Wash waved the black handset.

The old men were both behind the counter downstairs.

Oodles could hear the ring tone going on and on. "Maybe they're deep sleepers, which might explain why they didn't hear the noise last night."

A raspy voice came up from the floor of the foyer. "What fucking noise?"

Oodles looked over at Moose on his makeshift bed. "I already told you. Someone has stolen the Colonel Robert Northan statue."

Moose levered himself up. "The statue? Really? I was so sleepy when you woke me up, I couldn't work out why you were so worked up that *Jimbo* Northan was missing, when I knew Wish-Wash already knew that."

"Did Joffa mention he was going somewhere?" Wish-Wash asked Moose as he hobbled towards them.

"Not that I recall," Moose said. "I can tell you this though. Joffa is no heavy sleeper. You don't spend the years inside he has without learning to sleep with one eye open."

———

Wish-Wash and Oodles wondered if Joffa and Katy's buzzer was even working because it made no sound as they pressed the button next to the door.

The couple lived in the flat above the salon in the centre of town.

"It might be ringing upstairs, and we just can't hear it," Oodles said as they waited. And rang. And waited. And rang. And waited.

"Joffa would have said if he was going away?" Wish-Wash said. "He's due to take Awesome Sauce out bush this morning."

"One thing's for certain." Oodles looked up at the dark clouds overhead. "You can't send the kid out alone. Bad enough he'd get himself lost. But he also might drown."

"It'd make a man out of him."

"It'd make his grandfather very mad if we lose him."

Wish-Wash rang the doorbell again. "We'd just deny he was ever here. Now the pub's burned down, no one can prove he even was."

"His fingerprints would be all over the museum."

Wish-Wash glared at Oodles, and held his finger on the door bell for ages. Finally, he said, "Looks like we're wasting valuable time here. They've obviously gone. Possibly kidnapped too. We'll have to call in the police. If Stretch is still away, maybe his wife can contact him by radio."

———————

But Stretch was back. He hadn't shaved when he answered the door dressed in his pyjamas.

"Oodles, Wish-Wash . . . do you know what time it is?" He looked at his watch, which indicated he didn't know either. "Sheesh, I've only been asleep for two hours."

"We wouldn't wake you at this time of day you unless it was urgent," Oodles said. "We knew you'd want to know someone has stolen the statue."

Stretch rubbed sleep from one eye. "The statue?"

"The Colonel Northan statue," Oodles said.

"Yeah, right? Has April Fool's Day come early this year?"

"Come and look for yourself."

Stretch yawned. "Hang on, I'll get my dressing gown."

He returned 30 seconds later wrapped in a white towelling robe. "OK, let's take a look." He waggled a finger. "But if this is your idea of a joke . . . "

When they reached the street, he looked to the right and gasped.

"Well, I'll be . . . " He stared at the spot where the statue used to be. It was starting to rain.

"You or Elaine didn't hear anything?" Oodles said.

Stretch rubbed both eyes with his knuckles and looked at the void again. "Elaine has gone to her mother's, and I only got back from Bing Bong Mountain around 3am."

"You didn't happen to see Joffa and Katy up there, I don't suppose?" Oodles said.

"What?" Stretch said. "You know what happened the last time Joffa went fly-fishing? I don't think he'd expose Katy to those risks?"

"They've got to be somewhere. Wish-Wash and I can't raise them at their flat."

"They might have been kidnapped!" Wish-Wash blurted.

Stretch rolled his eyes. "First, James Northan. Now Joffa and Katy! You need to calm down, Wish-Wash. There is usually a logical explanation for people's disappearances." He shook his head slowly. "The missing statue requires more thought though. I should have known something was wrong though when I saw it was dark when I drove in. Someone must have cut the street lights."

Oodles frowned. "But you didn't see anyone? Messerschmitt, for instance?"

"Messerschmitt? You're trying to pin this one on him too?"

Wish-Wash stamped a foot, which sent splatters of muddy water on to the bottom of Stretch's dressing gown. "Why else would he have been measuring the statue with a tape yesterday? Oodles helped him." He looked at the other old man. "Didn't you?"

Oodles coughed into his hand. "Help is not exactly the right word. He threatened to strangle Gough unless I held the tape."

Stretch brightened. "Now *that* I can work with. The courts take a dim view of those type of threats. But did he say *why* he was measuring the statue?"

Oodles shook his head, showering the others in water. The rain was getting heavy now.

Stretch ushered them to the shelter of a roadside tree.

"It's all very circumstantial," Stretch said. "He can claim all kinds of reasons for measuring it."

Oodles looked him in the eye. "Like what?"

"He might have been sizing it up for a Halloween costume."

"Bit late, isn't it?" Oodles said.

"Or early," Wish-Wash added.

"Of all the things Messerschmitt's been accused of, intelligence isn't one of them," Stretch said.

Wish-Wash rasped the whiskers on his cheek with a palm. "So you won't even talk to him?"

"I didn't say that." Stretch tightened his dressing gown cord. "We need to get in out of this rain and I need to conduct my own investigation."

He lowered his voice. "Just between us — and I don't want this blabbed back to me in The Wind Tunnel Cafe — I need to interview him anyway. I was in radio contact with my constables yesterday and they're pretty sure an accelerant was used at the seat of the fire at the pub."

Wish-Wash looked into Oodles's eyes. "Told you."

Stretch made a downward movement with his hands. "Don't get too excited. Far as I can gather, there are no witnesses. My boys were unable to track Messerschmitt down and assumed he had gone into hiding. But now you're telling me, Oodles, you saw him at the statue?"

"Have you checked Stalag 79?" Wish-Wash said.

Stretch looked at him blankly.

"Messerschmitt's fibro cottage in Hill Street. That's where we think he's holding Jimbo."

Stretch shook his head slowly. "Yes, you said last week. And do you remember what I said? We just can't go searching premises without evidence."

When Oodles and Wish-Wash got back to the museum, the first thing they saw was Gough still tied to the post, lapping water from the gutter. The second thing they saw was Awesome Sauce wearing oversized yellow oilskins coming out through the front door.

"Moose lent his wet-weather gear to me," the American kid explained as he passed them.

It made no sense him going outside into the heavy rain when they were keen to get in out of the elements. Once inside, they turned and could see him through the window raising his face to the sky, water coming off him like a water-wheel.

Moose laughed behind them. "I told him he had to go outside and acclimatise!" He stopped chuckling. "Problem is, I can't see Joffa even wanting to go out in this weather — which means it's probably only a dress rehearsal."

Wish-Wash grimaced. "We think Joffa's also gone missing."

"Joffa's Mr Reliable," Moose said. "He'll be here."

"You reckon? Not only was he not answering his phone, he wasn't answering his doorbell."

"What are you saying?" Moose said.

The door opened and in came Awesome Sauce. His hair was saturated, and he shook himself off at the door, spraying the floor with water.

"Gawdsake!" Oodles said. "I'm not sure who looks more like a drowned rat? You or my soggy doggy out there."

"You haven't forgotten him, then?" the kid asked.

"No, I'll be taking Gough home to his kennel as soon as this rain eases."

If Awesome Sauce heard Oodles, he didn't acknowledge it. He was too busy opening the door for the incoming flash of yellow.

————

"You've escaped!" Wish-Wash cried.

"Escaped?" Joffa looked from face to face. "What the feck are you talking about? What's going on? I just walked past the statue of the Big Gobshite, only it's gone."

"We thought they must have had you too?" Wish-Wash said.

"*Had* me? Who?"

"Whoever nicked the statue last night. Messerschmitt's men probably."

"I wasn't even in Windy Mountain last night."

"You didn't tell me you were going away?" Moose said.

"Katy surprised me with a trip to the coast for the night. I don't know when all this happened? But I know we were fooling around on the beach at midnight." He scratched his backside. "I've got sand grit to prove it."

"Told you he'd be here," Moose said to the others.

"The way I see it, this is the best way to beat everyone to that Toiger," Joffa said. "Show ponies don't like going out in the rain. But us Irishmen are used to a bit of drizzle."

Oodles pointed out the window. "Are you sure you want to take a rookie out on such a dirty day?"

Joffa looked Awesome Sauce up and down "Looks like you're also eager to go?"

The Texan nodded. "A bit of rain never hurt anyone. Ask the very first member of the Noah family."

Moose hobbled over and slapped Joffa on the back. "I've packed the radios in Awesome Sauce's backpack. I've tuned them into the right frequency now, so you've got no excuse for not keeping in touch."

———

The room fell silent when Joffa and Awesome Sauce left.

Moose, Wish-Wash and Oodles stood in the foyer staring out the streaming windows.

The first bus of the day was an hour away, so there was no rush to take up their positions.

Oodles was imagining all the things that could go wrong. You wouldn't send your worst enemy bush out in this weather. The Bing Bong River was probably already starting to run fast up the mountain, visibility would drop to nearly zero with all the mist, even the rugged wet-weather gear they were wearing wouldn't keep Joffa and Awesome Sauce dry, and good luck trying to start a campfire.

He finally broke the silence. "I'm not sure we've thought this through very well. What if they do catch a Tasmanian Tiger? Won't it give the Noah family some ownership?"

"You worry too much." Wish-Wash got up and headed towards the stairs. "I am just going upstairs, and may be some time."

"Don't pretend you're Captain Oates. That's just code for you're going to have a smoke in the dunny, isn't it?" Oodles said.

Moose grinned. "You'd better be quick, Wish-Wash. In this weather those boys would be lucky to see their hands in front of their faces — especially Awesome Sauce with those glasses. I reckon they'll radio soon asking for permission to come home."

Wish-Wash was starting to climb the stairs when the phone began ringing. He shook his head as he turned around.

Moose shrugged. "So I was wrong about them using the radio. They're obviously ringing from Joffa's mobile phone instead."

Wish-Wash picked up the phone and sounded surprised. "Sergeant Stretch? Something else we can help you with?" This is when he started to go pale. "Really? Yes, um, we will be there as soon as we can."

When he hung up, Oodles said, "Let me guess? Stretch saw Joffa and Awesome Sauce walking past the cop shop heading towards the mountain track, and he's worried?"

Wish-Wash shook his head.

Oodles offered his next theory. "He's tracked down Messerschmitt then and is inviting us to help interrogate him?"

Wish-Wash shook his head again. "You won't believe this but Jimbo has just walked into the police station."

ELEVEN
KILLING US SOFTLY

JAMES LOOKED up from his bed when Sergeant Stretch opened the cell door.

"I'll leave you two to catch up with Sergeant Shultz," Stretch said, with an emphasis on *Sergeant Shultz*. "Sorry, but I have to lock the door behind you. Just give me a hoy when you're done."

James stood as Stretch disappeared through the outer door, which he left ajar.

The Mayor was dressed as usual in his three-piece suit but for once no briefcase was in sight.

"I would offer you both a chair but as you can see . . . " James looked around. "Shame that leaky toilet has no lid. I guess you will just have to sit on the other bed."

"We can't do that! We're drenched." Oodles said.

James sighed dramatically. "With any luck, it will just dilute the smell of wee. That stench has nothing to do with me, I might add."

Wish-Wash sat down on the empty bed, which was so close to James's their knees touched. "You're *Sergeant Shultz*! What's going on, Jimbo?"

"I gave myself up, did I not?" James intently adjusted one of his hearing aids and it made a high-pitch shrill. "I have been hiding out at my nephew's."

Oodles motioned for Wish-Wash to shift over and make room for him to sit down. "I never knew you even had a nephew, old cock?"

"Jonny Northan? He lives in a fibro cottage in Hill Street."

Wish-Wash's eyes popped. "Messerschmitt? He's your nephew?"

James stood up. "Would *you* tell anyone you were related to him? He is one of the black sheep of a family that, frankly," — he pivoted and nodded towards the dripping cistern in the corner — "is going down the toilet."

"That doesn't explain why you did a disappearing act?" Oodles said.

James pointed a finger at Wish-Wash. "This is all your fault!"

"You're blaming me! How's it my fault?"

"If you had not talked me into that confounded DNA test . . . "

This brought out the bush lawyer in Oodles, who levered himself to his feet, with the help of a hand on the bed to keep his balance. "As I recall, James, you were the one who talked Wish-Wash into taking the test. What happened? Did you find out you're not related to Shakespeare?"

James sat back down, threw his head into his hands and started sobbing.

When he lifted his head, he had a stream of tears running down his nose. He reached into his pocket for his white, monogrammed handkerchief and blew his nose loudly. "I should have listened to you, Clarence. Only *you* refused to do the test." He looked daggers at Wish-Wash. "If *you* had refused, I would have not gone through it alone."

"What's it blinking matter?" Oodles resumed his seat. "So what if you're not related to a famous Englishman!" He pointed to the wall beyond which the statue used to be. "You can still lay claim to being a descendant of Colonel Richard Northan."

This brought more tears. "You fail to understand, Clarence. When I got my DNA test back I thought, no, that cannot be right. So I did a little research to prove my result wrong."

Oodles examined his motley face. "And?"

"Turns out the damn test was right. Oh, the shame, the shame." He buried his head again. When he came up for air, he said: "Do you not understand? Richard Northan was Irish. Bog Irish. He was a pauper's son from County Donegal who was transported to Van Diemen's Land for seven years for theft. He never even rode a horse. I ought to have suspected something was amiss. I grew up looking at an oil painting of him hanging in the study and it was all wrong."

"What was wrong about it?"

"He had three chins and looked like Ronnie Corbett sitting in an oversized chair. He bore no resemblance to the dashing figure on horseback that stood in the High Street! That *flagitium hominis!*"

He hid his head in his hands until he gathered himself again. "The shame. The shame. Even when he was foreman of the work gang that settled Windy Mountain, and probably built this very building, they would have clapped him in a ball and chain at night. Even if he joined the forces after serving his time, the best rank he could have risen to would have been sergeant. So where the *colonel* came from, I know not."

Wish-Wash stood up and did a little jig between the beds. "What a happy coincidence, Jimbo! My DNA test also shows my roots are in Donegal! You know what this means? We might well be related! Cuz!"

James groaned and plunged his head back into his hands. "I knew it, I just knew it." He raised his head again. "I should have drowned myself in the sewerage ponds when I had the chance."

"So you *were* there?" Wish-Wash said.

"I'm surprised you didn't see Jonny and Spot on the way there, Bert."

"Spot? Who's Spot?"

"I can't bring myself to call him Adolf any more than I can bear to call his master Messerschmitt."

"And you put up that doctored sign?"

"I helped. Jonny and I carried it all the way from town. But then he left me to do my bit. He needed someone literate to rework it."

"You mean he can't spell?" Wish-Wash said.

"He's done well with his business despite being dyslexic." He looked to see if they recognised the name. "Jonno's Rleocation Service?"

Oodles and Wish-Wash looked at each other. "Them!" Wish-Wash grunted.

James nodded. "Jonny is not involved in the company day-to-day. But when he sends them a fax, they just follow orders."

"So you've been behind all this? All this time we were blaming Messerschmitt. You told him to burn down the pub too?"

"Not that!" James's delivery came with a shower of snot. "That really was Jonny's idea. I knew nothing about it till an hour ago. All I was interested in was removing everything in this town associated with that Big *Flagitium Hominis*."

Wish-Wash looked at him quizzically. "There are those words again? I must have missed that Shakespearean play."

"It's not Shakespeare. It's the latin term for *disgraceful man*. That's what it's come to for a once-glorious statue."

James smiled for the first time. "The old boy network came in handy. Manky Manning was very happy to take the bench off my hands."

The smile turned into a snarl. "But that's when I started to suspect Jonny was both psychotic and narcissistic. I advised him mostly strongly against putting a plaque on the bench and drawing attention to himself, but would he listen!"

He held up his finger and thumb a half inch apart. "Mind you, I had a close call the day you went to *The Pick of the Crop* office. Jonny and Spot had already left to walk back into town, but I was still there with a paintbrush. I was amazed you didn't see me scampering across the road and hiding in the bushes."

"But the pub?" Wish-Wash said.

James's voice sank to a low croak again. "I didn't know anything about that. I heard about it, of course, but I just assumed it was an accident. For me, the crowning glory was the removal of the Big *Flagitium*

Hominis in the middle of the night. Everything went like clockwork. We had already ensured that Sergeant Stretch had left town for a few days. That was easy. I dropped an anonymous note into his letterbox saying the fish were biting up at Bing Bong Mountain. I had to give some more thought into luring away the only two other residents in the area. I dropped a voucher into Katy and Joffa's letterbox giving them a free romantic get-away for one night down the coast. The demolition crew was brilliant. After cutting off the street lights, they worked like a well-oiled machine in the dark." He flashed a smile.

"He was going to offload the statue on to Slutz Plains Council, wasn't he?" Oodles said.

"No, that was a false trail. The silly boy told me he had put that idea in your head. It was his idea of a joke, I think, but in my mind it was a mistake to draw attention to himself again. The truth was I had lined up a discreet buyer on the mainland."

"But the pub! Why did he burn down the pub?" Wish-Wash cried.

James blinked slowly. "Who knows how these morons think? My guess is Jonny is from the most Irish reaches of the family. He got it into his head that if he burned down the pub, he would be able to buy the land for a song."

Oodles and Wish-Wash exchanged glances.

"My fault, really. I probably planted the seed in his defective brain. With bits of the town disappearing, I told him people would start leaving in droves, which meant he would be able to buy up whole swathes of the town cheaply until he owned the majority of it, and he really liked the idea of renaming it Appletown. But I nearly choked on my cornflakes when he told me at breakfast today he had actually burned down the pub. He was even proud of it. He even asked me what did I think of the name The Burnt Apple, which he was going to call the rebuild."

James shook his head, spraying Oodles with tears and more mucus. "Relocating town landmarks is one thing, but I wanted no part of arson. That is why I turned myself in." He looked around at his spartan surroundings. "And this is the thanks I get?"

Wish-Wash looked around. "The old cells were in much poorer nick. What does Stretch say will happen now?"

James bowed his head and spoke to his knees. "No matter I have given myself up, no matter I have given him his only solid evidence Jonny burned down the hotel, he is threatening to throw the book at me too. I think what has really got under his skin was my impersonating a police officer when I told *The Pick of the Crop* you had both been killed in that accident."

Wish-Wash groaned. "Killing us is a bit extreme, even for you, Jimbo."

Oodles gasped. "Why would you even do that?"

"Is it not obvious? I was trying to discredit *The Pick of the Crop* as a newspaper that has never checked its facts. That sorry excuse for a newspaper is to blame for building up the fake reputation of Richard Northan."

James looked around at the spartan surroundings again. "Anyone would think I am a criminal!"

"I guess it's up to a court of law to rule otherwise," Oodles said.

James blinked away more tears. "I could be locked up for weeks waiting for my day in court."

"Months probably, Jimbo," Wish-Wash said. "Which is a pity. I have no idea if we're allowed to send postcards to remand prisoners."

James looked from face to face, and his mouth crinkled. "Postcards? Where are you going?"

Oodles gave a nervous little cough. "We would have told you sooner if you hadn't disappeared. You know that DNA test? You know it had a prize of a holiday? The one you said was just made up to get people in? Wish-Wash won it. He's taking me to Ireland with him."

Wish-Wash reached over and squeezed James's knee. "I wish there was a mirror in here so you could see the look on your face. Why don't you go see if you can see your reflection in the dunny pan?"

Oodles shrugged. "Now I think about it, I can't see how you two could be related. I mean, you said, James, that Richard Northan was a pauper's son. Wish-Wash, on the other hand, has just inherited a castle in County Donegal."

James jumped to his feet. "A castle!" he shrieked.

When the words finished ricocheting around the cell, Wish-Wash said, "I couldn't believe it either." He locked on to James's eyes. "Tell you what? If you somehow get out of this fix you're in, we're taking you with us." He glanced at Oodles. "Isn't that right, cobber?"

"But we've only got two seats?"

"Two business-class seats. I'm sure they'll cash them in for three economy seats."

————

When they got back on to the street, Oodles said, "Why did you have to go and tell him that?"

"Torture!" Wish-Wash laughed as he opened the orange umbrella on the footpath. "Jimbo is going down."

Oodles glared at him as the rain pelted down. "We don't know that for sure?"

"Sure we do." Wish-Wash huddled under the umbrella. "Here, come in out of the wet. Nobody fakes their own kidnap and steals the landmarks he's stolen, and gets away with it. You heard what Stretch said as we were leaving. He's confident they'll find Messerschmitt and put him away. But for his part, Jimbo has to be looking at two years at least."

"You have more faith in the legal system than me, old cock."

"Relax, Oodles. Think about all the postcards we can send him?"

Wish-Wash turned and headed up the street, taking the umbrella with him and leaving Oodles without cover again.

"Hey," Oodles shouted. "Aren't you going the wrong way?"

Wish-Wash turned. "Oh, I forgot. I told Moose to hold the fort but I forgot to tell you. I'm catching the bus up to Slutz Plains. Be back this arvo." He strode off towards the bus shelter.

———

Seven hours later, Wish-Wash approached the museum with an umbrella in one hand and the handle of a green carry-bag in the other.

Oodles and Moose raced to open the door. Even though he only had one good leg, Moose won.

Wish-Wash frowned as he stepped into the foyer, shook his umbrella and closed it. "No one usually opens the door for me. What's up?"

"We've got a bit of news you'll want to hear." Moose looked back to Oodles. "You want to tell him?"

"Only if he tells us what he's got in the bag," Oodles said.

Wish-Wash looked down at the bag hanging from his left hand. "If you must know, I've brought back Rod's baby book, OK? I have a few years to catch up on."

"Strewth!" Oodles said. "What did he say when you got off the bus dressed in that soggy Hawaiian shirt?"

"Snap."

"Snap?"

"I thought I had the only Hawaiian shirt in this region." Wish-Wash put his umbrella down near the door, walked to the counter and leaned over and put the bag on the other side, before turning around. "Turns out Rod has one just like it. What are the odds of him wearing it today!"

"I thought his name was Roderick?"

"It is, but we did a deal. He hates being called Roderick. But he wanted to call me Pop, so we agreed on Rod and Wish-Wash."

"You're letting him call you Wish-Wash?" Oodles's voice came out all croaky, like he was running out of breath. "How is he ever going to learn to respect you?"

"I think he already looks up to me. I think he sees me as some kind of fashion guru who has already blazed the trail for him."

"Gawd help us." Oodles looked up to the ceiling.

Wish-Wash cocked his ear. "I can't hear the kettle boiling?"

"You only just came in," Oodles said. "Don't you want to hear the news?"

"Tell you the truth, I've had so much news today I'm not sure if my ticker is up to more goss."

"Yeah, but this isn't bad news like James being in jail," Oodles said.

"I'd rate that as *good* news." Wish-Wash looked to Moose. "You'd agree with me, right?" He smiled. "It's a wonder I didn't see dancing in the street when I was walking back from the bus stop. I'd reckon a lot of people in Windy Mountain have been waiting for this day."

Oodles looked at him darkly. "You shouldn't be dancing on his grave."

Wish-Wash's grin became broader. "I've still got that celebration to look forward to, have I? I didn't think we still had the death penalty!"

"I give up," Oodles said. "Do you want to know or don't you?"

"Only over a cuppa. I'm parched after the bus trip." He raised his voice so V over the other side of the foyer could hear. "I need a drink. And a bickie."

Oodles pointed to a chair. "You're going to have to sit down to hear this."

Wish-Wash sat, but raised a hand when Oodles went to speak again. "It's been a very demanding day. Tea first, and then I'll listen."

"Have it your own way." Oodles looked at the front windows still being lashed with rain. "I guess there is no hurry."

V delivered afternoon tea on a tray.

"Are you ready?" Oodles didn't wait for an answer. He slapped his knees. "They've done it!"

"Who's done what?" Wish-Wash said.

"Joffa and Awesome Sauce have trapped that Tasmanian Tiger. They were on the CB radio just now."

Wish-Wash looked at Moose, who had sat down opposite. "I thought you said you had tracked it to the other side of Bing Bong Mountain. They couldn't possibly have gone that far yet."

Moose shrugged. "I guess I was wrong about the weather stopping them. Who knew the Tiger would also track back this way? Apparently, it wandered into their campsite when they stopped for lunch, and Joffa threw a net over it."

"Really?" Wish-Wash said. "It came to them? This shy, nocturnal animal that hasn't been verified for how many years just gives itself up like Jimbo did?"

Moose squirmed a little in his chair. "Let me tell you, I was also sceptical. But Joffa says he's 100 per cent sure, and Awesome Sauce agrees."

"Oh, *Awesome Sauce* agrees, does he?" Wish-Wash said. "Why doesn't that fill me with confidence?"

"You're too hard on that kid," Oodles said. "I just hope you're going to put on a big smile when you pose with him for all the press."

"What? When?"

"I need to ring around all the major newspapers and TV news people. It's too wet and slippery to attempt the trip in fading light, so Joffa and Awesome Sauce are coming out at first light tomorrow." He stood up and went to the back of Wish-Wash and patted his clammy Hawaiian shirt. "It's show time."

TWELVE
WE GOTTA GET OUT OF THIS PLACE
WEDNESDAY MORNING, 11.20

"I THOUGHT you said they'd be here by now." Norm Hit looked at his watch. "Only I have more show results to type up back at the office."

One of the TV people also moaned. "At this rate, we're going to miss the lunchtime news."

The rain had stopped.

But the two dozen media people were getting ansty because they had been waiting in the museum car park with their cameras and fluffy microphones for almost two hours.

"I promise you they'll be here," Oodles said. "I bet they're being extra careful coming down the slippery paths. I'm sure you'll agree this is an event worth waiting for. I'm sure none of you wants to miss feasting your eyes on a real, live Tasmanian Tiger?"

He had them by the short and curlies there. This odd marsupial had really captured imaginations for generations. They were on the precipice of the scoop of the century.

"Look." A member of the media pack pointed up the road. "Here they come."

The cage hung from a pole. Joffa carried the front bit and Awesome

Sauce had the rear. As they came closer, Oodles could see the cage had been covered with wet-weather gear.

Joffa and Awesome Sauce were smiling like returning heroes when they lowered the cage carefully to the ground.

Oodles looked at Wish-Wash to give him his cue.

Wish-Wash, resplendent in red trousers and a lime-green polo shirt, stepped forward and adopted the voice of a ring master.

"Ladies and gentlemen, prepare to be amazed."

He grabbed a handful of the yellow wet-weather gear on top of the cage and pulled it off as he said. "I give you, the Tasmanian Tiger."

Excited eyes homed in on the cage. Their facial expressions turned to disappointment and disbelief just as fast.

Oodles pinched the bridge of his nose.

Wish-Wash shook his head.

To be fair to Joffa and Awesome Sauce, it was a big specimen: two-and-a-half feet with a bushy tail almost as long.

But it wasn't a Tasmanian Tiger, not even close. Its body was spotted, not striped. They had actually captured a large native cat.

THIRTEEN
COME FLY WITH ME
TWENTY DAYS LATER

OODLES LEANT on his new walking stick as he watched Rod lift the suitcase into the back of the dual-cab ute. "It's very good of you to pick me up from home."

"Not a problem, Mr Noodle." He clipped up the tarpaulin.

The big day had arrived. Wish-Wash's new grandson had offered to drive them to the airport near Launceston. From there, they'd fly to Melbourne. Then Melbourne to Dubai. Then Dubai to London. Then London to Dublin. Then by road to Donegal.

Rod was dressed in lime-green trousers and a blue polo shirt with a red hoop around his midriff.

Oodles went to the back door behind the driver's seat. "I'll let your pop sit in the front when we pick him up at the museum."

Rod's voice rose sharply behind him. "Don't let him hear you call him that!"

"I know. He won't be happy. But at my age, you have to take pleasures when you can get them." Oodles chuckled as he sat on the edge of the seat and swung his legs in.

He hadn't had much to laugh about these past couple of weeks.

First, Doc Jenkins had issued him with a caveat. "No walking stick, no travel." Oodles didn't feel he needed a stick, and he certainly didn't want to tell Wish-Wash he needed one.

In the end though, events wore him down to the point he realised he really was getting older, and to hell with the *hee-haw, hee-haw* derision.

The media had hung him and Wish-Wash out to dry. Joffa and Awesome Sauce escaped the worst of the ridicule, it was the old men who got it in the neck.

In desperation, Oodles had asked Awesome Sauce if Tim Noah Junior would still be interested in buying the place.

"Didn't I tell you Granddaddy is in a nursing home?" Awesome Sauce said.

"Is he?" Oodles said. "Oh, I am sorry. But who's taken over the bushranger whiskers import business?"

"My father. Tim Noah the Third."

"Would he be interested in buying the museum?"

Awesome Sauce shook his head. "Daddy was the one who sent me off to see the world. He says he doesn't want to see me again until I've made my Fortune. Last time I tried to Skype him, he blocked me."

Oodles and Wish-Wash decided the best thing to do was just walk away. They gifted the museum to Moose, Joffa and Katy. As soon as Moose got the plaster off, he would be moving back into the flat above the museum. Katy planned to give up her hairdressing job to become the new manager at the museum, which would allow Moose and Joffa to team up as trackers again. Awesome Sauce had agreed to stay on in the single bed. Everyone at the museum had agreed to share looking after Gough while the old men were away.

As Rod backed out of the drive, he half-turned his head. "You know Wish-Wash has agreed to come and live with me in Slutz Plains."

"No way," Oodles gasped. "I thought he planned to move back into the pub now Rog's decided to rebuild it."

"I think he was waiting for the right time to tell you about his new plan. Between you and I, I think he wants to get right away from James Northan."

"Strewth! How far away from James does he want to be? Risdon Prison is a long way away from Windy Mountain. It's just a crying shame the police weren't able to track down that nephew of his. No one would mess with James if Messerschmitt was his cellmate."

"Didn't Wish-Wash tell you?" Rod said. "James Northan has been released. The council didn't want to press charges. And Sergeant Stretch changed his mind about charging him with impersonating a police officer." Oodles saw the back of Rod shrugging. "Turns out impersonating a TV actor isn't actually a crime."

"You're kidding me?" Oodles watched the houses whizz past as they drove down the hill. "He stole the signs, Gawdsake; he gave away *our* bench; he stole the statue. Doesn't that count for anything?"

"Mayor Maddie Northan reckons he had council permission to do all those things," Rod said.

"What about the attempt to relocate the museum? James was behind that!"

"He says he wasn't. It's his word against Messerschmitt's — and he's obviously not here."

Oodles shook his head.

"You know Wish-Wash is giving up the cigarettes?" Rod said.

"Nooooo?"

"Yes, indeedy. Someone told him they eject smokers from the plane in mid-air?"

"What a rotten thing for someone to say!"

———

Two men were standing with suitcases on the footpath outside the museum. One was dressed in an emerald green suit, the other bloke was James Northan.

Oodles undid his seatbelt and got out, as did Rod.

Oodles took Wish-Wash aside and whispered in his ear. "Tell me he's not coming with us to Ireland!"

Wish-Wash smiled. "He's agreed to come along as our carer." He turned to face the Mayor and spoke loudly. "I do hope you've turned your hearing aids on, Jimbo?"

Rod unclipped the tarp and his hand moved towards the handle of the first suitcase to hoist it aboard.

But Wish-Wash reached out and stopped him. "That's Jimbo's job."

———

When they were all buckled into their seats, James asked who was going to be looking after the museum in their absence.

Wish-Wash turned his head towards the back seat. "Didn't we tell you? Those jail walls used to have ears in my day."

"This will be tedious trip, Bert, if you're going to bring that up again and again." James said. "Can't you give me a simple answer to a simple question?"

Wish-Wash scratched the stray whiskers on his neck. "Not that it's any of your business, Jimbo, but Joffa, Katy and Moose are taking over."

"Moose! You're joking. The museum will be lucky to be in one piece when you return."

Wish-Wash stretched his arm out over the top of Rod's headrest. "Doesn't matter to us, does it Oodles? We've retired again. We've handed over the deeds to them on a permanent basis so it's their business to deal with now."

James rolled his eyes. "What could go wrong?"

Lots, as it turns out.

But that's a story for the next book in the Windy Mountain series.

NEXT IN THE WINDY MOUNTAIN SERIES

Even when they're not there, the old men are complicating things. Find out how in Book 3.

Oodles, Wish-Wash and the Mayor have gone to Ireland to research family history, and have washed their hands of the Tasmanian Tiger Museum.

But the new owners are thrown into a puzzle after a garden ornament goes missing.

The clues include a skeleton, a chess set, and a concrete marsupial with a secret pouch.

The old men are no help. In fact, their emails just muddy the waters.

EMAIL FROM DUBLIN

KATY LIFTED her head from the computer screen when she heard tapping on the front window.

It was Sergeant Stretch! What was so urgent at this time of the morning?

Katy hadn't even had time to clear away yesterday afternoon's six empty cups, let alone open up the museum.

She went to the door, unlatched it, and let the policeman in.

He just grunted and walked past her to the counter, where he laid down his cap. He turned around, and slowly panned the foyer with squinty eyes as if he was going to stride over to one of the dirty cups and issue it with a defect notice.

He made a clicking noise with his tongue as he shook his head. "I hope you know what you are taking on, little lady?" Then he breathed out loudly. "I'm actually here on official business."

Katy rolled her eyes. "What's Moose supposed to have done now?" She had cut Stretch's hair for twenty years, so she was well aware of the bad blood between him and Moose. Moose was a man mountain who quite literally was the state's biggest expert on the Tasmanian Tiger, but he had also done some time in jail where his size had been both an asset and a curse. He had been so happy yesterday to finally get his plaster cast off and walk without the aid of crutches. This was going to turn his mood south again.

"Not him, *this time!*" Stretch ran a hand through his hair, which was longer than usual. "I was hoping to get some background information on the old couple who moved into Messerschmitt's old place in Hill Street. Mr and Mrs le Blanc? Know them?"

"Should I?"

"I thought you might have cut their hair."

"No, I haven't. Have you asked Vicki or Velda?"

Stretch gave the smallest of head shakes as he reached into his pocket and pulled out a roll of peppermints. "Messerschmitt never actually owned the house. It was rented out to him by you know who. When he did a runner, she had the place cleared out so it could go back on the rental market."

"What has the old couple done?" Katy asked.

Stretch unwrapped the mints and offered her one. The strong smell, mingled with the scent of his cheap aftershave, made her gag and she waved the offer away.

He kept holding out the roll. "Sure? Are you feeling all right? You look a bit pale."

He popped a mint into his mouth and started aggressively sucking it before locking eyes with Katy again. "This is just between you and I, right? It's not what the old couple have done. Quite the reverse. Someone has kidnapped one of the concrete dwarfs from their garden."

"Kids playing a prank?"

"That was my first thought," he said in a stream of minty breath. "But would kids go to the trouble of leaving a handwritten ransom note? Do children even get taught Cord Cursive any more?"

"Perhaps the kidnapper thinks Messerschmitt still lives there?" Katy said.

Stretch started crunching the mint as he considered this. "Unlikely," he said when he had swallowed. "Messerschmitt's dog kept a nicer garden than him. At least Adolf dug some holes."

Stretch's voice became more relaxed — less formal. "Heard from the old blokes?"

Katy pointed to the computer on the other side of the grey, laminated counter. "The email I just got from them said they were about to pick up a hire car to drive from Dublin to Donegal."

Stretch clicked his tongue again. "I don't envy the Irish traffic police. I presume Oodles is driving?"

Katy looked up at him. "Wish-Wash has never had a licence, and no one around here can remember the Mayor driving."

"Oh, I bet Moose can. Sergeant Smith was dead-set certain it was him who slashed the Mayor's tyres all those years ago. He just couldn't prove it."

James Northan, a.k.a. the Mayor, hadn't actually been the mayor for some time but he was descended from Colonel Richard Northan, whose forebears had dominated the office since he founded the town in 1841. The mayoral chains now hung around the neck of James's daughter Maddie. She also headed the family trust that owned half the real estate in town, including the hairdressing salon she had just bought from Katy for her adopted daughters.

Stretch turned his head when he heard vehicles pulling up outside. The pitch of his voice rose as he slipped back into officious mode. "Are those tradies from the building site next door parking their utes in your car park? Want me to go tell them to move?"

"They're not harming anyone," Katy said. "They make the museum look busier than it is."

"Someone has to tell them they're trespassing." He was halfway to the door when the rungs on the staircase at the back of the room began reverberating.

Stretch looked around to see Moose limping down the final steps, scratching the hairy belly behind his unbuttoned shirt.

The bearded man locked eyes with Stretch.

"Nice bald spot you've got going there, Sergeant," Moose said.

Stretch looked like a tomato in a stiff blue uniform as he returned to collect his cap, which he slammed on his head before turning. "Some of us have proper work to do." He banged the glass door behind him.

AUTHOR'S NOTE

MY GREAT, great, great grandfather was a cobbler from County Tyrone, just across the river from County Donegal — so I lie in bed awake at night wondering if perhaps I am related to Wish-Wash.

Yes, I know Wish-Wash is really a fiction character but logic goes out the window when you're half-asleep!

As we get older, it's probably natural to pay more interest to our family tree: to want to know where we came from. DNA testing was all the rage in my circle of family and friends when I was writing this book.

I know some readers were disappointed the old men didn't actually make it to Donegal in this novel.

All I can say is "patience".

It took Wish-Wash's ancestor many months to get to Australia on a wooden ship. He didn't have the comfort of an easy chair and a reading light either.

Take it from an Australian who has travelled the other way a few times. Even flying seems to take forever,

I don't even know if this book has reached Donegal yet.

Ireland does figure on sales charts for other books in the series —

along with about 80 other countries — but I don't receive a regional breakdown.

Give me a hoy if you're from Donegal.

FINALLY

This novel has been professionally edited. If you've got this far my guess is you've successfully navigated the Australian spelling, slang and deliberate oddities. But typos always manage to slip through the net, so by all means let me know if something's out of order.

– John Martin
https://johnmartin-author.blog

MY BOOKS

Windy Mountain series

Lie of the Tiger (#1)

He's not who he says he is. Who will rescue him?

———

Blokes on a Plane (#2)

Why is the mayor speaking old English? And where has he disappeared to?

———

Whitey and the Six Dwarfs (#3)

Troupe of Elvis impersonators come to the rescue.

———

Blokes in Donegal (#4)

Three old blokes go to Ireland hoping to discover family history. The mayor had to take his great, great, great grandfather's head, didn't he!

———

Blokes in the House (#5)

How the old blokes coped with COVID quarantine (clue: the major didn't).

———

Who Knew Tasmanian Tigers Eat Apples. (#6)

Back to before the beginning. Wish-Wash leads a public revolt.

———

Who Knew Tiger Sharks also Eat Apples? (#7)

A character from the old days returns in an unlikely guise. It's all about comic revenge.

———

The Life and Deaths of Billy Gumboots (#8)

'His foot, my boot.'

_____

Blokes Send in the Clones (#9)

Two old blokes have a crack at cloning a Tasmanian tiger.

To come:

10 — Blokes do the Block

Someone marries, someone dies. Might even be the same old bloke.

————

Funny Capers DownUnder series

The Wrong Magician (#1)

This time he has to make himself disappear.

———

Daddy's Great Escape (#2)

If Mad Bill hates people so much, why does he make it so hard for them to leave his island?

_____

Escape from Mad Bill's Island (#3)

He came seeking to find out what the British were up to on the island in World War 2. He won't like the answer.

———

Major B.S. comes to the end of his Rope

It all started when he rescued the wrong group of people from a prisoner-of-war camp. It just becomes worse.

———

www.ingramcontent.com/pod-product-compliance
Lightning Source LLC
Chambersburg PA
CBHW070929250626
47159CB00009B/3181